FATHER OF LIES

Also by Brian Evenson

Altmann's Tongue
A Collapse of Horses
Contagion
Dark Property
The Din of Celestial Birds
Fugue State
Immobility
Last Days
The Open Curtain
The Wavering Knife
Windeye

FATHER OF LIES

A Novel

Brian Evenson

Coffee House Press
Minneapolis
2016

First published in 1998 by Four Walls Eight Windows
Introduction © 2016 by Samuel R. Delany
Cover illustration and design by Sarah Evenson
Book design by Ann Sudmeier
Author photograph © Valerie Evenson

Coffee House Press books are available to the trade through our primary distributor, Consortium Book Sales & Distribution, cbsd.com or (800) 283-3572. For personal orders, catalogs, or other information, write to info@coffeehousepress.org.

Coffee House Press is a nonprofit literary publishing house. Support from private foundations, corporate giving programs, government programs, and generous individuals helps make the publication of our books possible. We gratefully acknowledge their support in detail in the back of this book.

LIBRARY OF CONGRESS CATALOGING-IN-PUBLICATION DATA

Evenson, Brian, 1966–
Father of lies : a novel / by Brian Evenson.
pages ; cm
ISBN 978-1-56689-415-9
1. Pedophilia—Fiction. 2. Church officers—Fiction.
3. Obedience—Religious aspects—Fiction. 4. Psychological fiction.
I. Title.
PS3555.V326F38 2016
813'.54—dc23
2015010555

PRINTED IN THE UNITED STATES OF AMERICA

INTRODUCTION

Brian Evenson's *Father of Lies*

by Samuel R. Delany

Father of Lies—Brian Evenson's first novel—might be called "patriarchal horror fiction." It deals with a situation conceivable in any hierarchical society where the head male has unquestioned institutional support for anything and everything he does, no matter whom he comes in conflict with, especially women and children. That authority derives from the fact that he is a man—regardless of what kind of man he is.

The book begins with a disturbing epigraph from the Kenyan novelist Ngũgĩ wa Thiong'o, in which a demon or god exhorts a father to slaughter and drink the blood of his favorite son. As I read it over, I asked myself: "Will Evenson be writing about a situation whose closeness in both space and time paradoxically enough emphasizes his and Thiong'o's cultural differences—in genre, in intent, in assumed psychology; in accessibility to one another and in politics—which is, in any case, a reading equally as ideological as the most traditional and racist, so that both of them must be interrogated with the greatest skepticism?"

But the fact is (partial disclosure . . .) I am re-reading Evenson's novel; I first read *Father of Lies* more than a decade back. I liked it then; I liked it this time. Sixteen-odd years ago I first heard Evenson read—in a white second-floor gallery room on Second Street, just below Market across from the Arden Theatre in Philadelphia. While we sat on our white enameled benches and black plastic chairs, Evenson read us a funny, moving, astutely observed story that was also an incisive dramatic analysis of an order of redneck buddy nutsiness—in the skids of Salt Lake. My response to his tale was one I've only had to a dozen-odd writers in my life: I want to know this one. Evenson has written a number of books between then and now, which I've also read and liked. Making it clearer where he has gone since makes it easier to see things that must have been important to him about the place he started out. And by this reading of the novel, I've learned a little more about him, both as a writer and as a person. Here's a bit of dialectic you can make of what you will. When, a couple of years after that first gallery reading, I finally read *Father of Lies,* page by page it did not produce as much pleasure as the earlier story. But the memory of the pleasure he'd produced and the skill he'd displayed were clear factors in making me trust what seemed a colder work to pay off by intellection what it lacked in laughs. The book rewards that trust. As well, in memory the first story was no less loaded with its own intellection. By now, as well, I've dedicated a novel of my own to Brian. (Disclosure, as they say, is full.)

For two years Brian Evenson served as a Mormon missionary in France and Switzerland. His BA was from Brigham Young University (BYU) in Provo, Utah. Then he went on for his MA and PHD at the University of Washington. In late 1993, with his wife and two daughters, he was again in Provo, preparing to teach at BYU. Earlier that year, five scholars from a group dubbed the "September Six" by the *Salt Lake Tribune* were excommunicated or disfellowshipped from Utah's Church of Jesus Christ of Latter-day Saints—generally known as Mormons—for publishing scholarly work allegedly criticizing or disagreeing with Mormon doctrine or church leadership. Evenson was friends with some in the group and sympathetic to many of their views.

A year later, still not thirty, Evenson's own first story collection, *Altmann's Tongue* (1994), appeared. A BYU student lodged a complaint with a Mormon church leader about the tales' violence and sexuality, which elicited a request from Evenson's department chair to Evenson that he write a response. When he did so, the chair sent it to university authorities and church leaders with an accompanying letter saying that Evenson had now been made to realize his stories were inappropriate and that he understood continuing to publish such work "would bring repercussions." When Evenson was shown the letter purporting to explain "his" feelings and what he now "understood," he began to feel that what he had thought was an honest request to explain his work was in fact a warning to stop writing what he was writing. This and similar incidents centering on two women colleagues at BYU prompted Evenson to end his relationship both with the educational institution and with the religion that supported it.

Before the *Altmann's Tongue* affair was over, Evenson began *Father of Lies*, aware it meant a break with a large part of his previous life and shifting beliefs till then. The idea for the novel had come as far back as his first term teaching at BYU, though he had been uncertain he would write it until he actually began.

Hearing from another writer about an opening at Oklahoma State that had not been filled because they were not happy with the candidates, Evenson sent in a late application, got the job, and left Provo, Utah, for Stillwater, Oklahoma, with his wife and daughters.

In 1996 in Oklahoma, Evenson completed *Father of Lies*. Not long after, he would resign from the Church of Jesus Christ of Latter-day Saints.

Most horror fiction is about evil—in much the same way most modern pornography tends to be about pleasure. But the horror or the pornography that does not end either as mindless uplift or with the most predictable condemnation of the transgressions, while it may or may not have some literary staying power, is pretty much excluded from any kind of broad or statistical mass popularity. Both are genres where, whether they know it or not, readers arrive wanting to know they'll be reassured at the end, one way or the other.

Evenson's novel is one where the boundary between them—horror and pornography—is unclear. Both are more implied than displayed.

When, observing the story or its organization from one direction, we turn up our critical focus, we can recognize that what is horrible is that someone or ones get pleasure from things most folks would find unpleasant or, even more, cruel and destructive—if not simply yucky.

When we move that heightened focus around to the other side of the same order of events, to look at the text's style or its emotional effect on us readers, it's equally clear that pleasure itself is a complex business. When we experience it ourselves, we recall certain biological reactions coupled with the ability to remember some of it, but we always emerge from it, even with the *aide-mémoire* of language and whatever sensory recall we can summon up, forgetful over time both of the experience and what we understood of it, a situation which appears to create a yearning to repeat. (Though it is introspective, this is still Freud's initial empirical evidence [see *The Ego and the Id,* 1915] for an Unconscious.) Here, what we experience and can observe, both in ourselves and in others, is desire, which Lacan describes as what remains when need is subtracted from want.

If we bring this critical focus back around to the evil itself—cruelty, destructiveness, the yucky—what we can see is the biological centrality of pain, discomfort, suffering; as well as the fear of them all and what they can grow into and what they all inevitably do grow into: death. Among the first questions experience leads us to ask is, in large institutional matters, how much of the same forgetfulness shapes not desire as a drive but as a barrier that resists any such drive and that must be overcome in order for the desires of most of the people to be achieved? What happens to the values of kindness and compassion of a small village church that will feed both the local indigent and the hungry wayfarer when they are displaced to a huge hospital in an undeveloped country—or, indeed, to an equally large hospital in a thriving capitalist city? "You can even come in—some of you—but we can't treat you, because we don't have the technology or you don't have the insurance or the money to pay us. Besides, we all die anyway, so what does it matter if it happens on a sidewalk outside because you are the wrong color or too poor or we don't have enough doctors: at any rate, we can make any of these excuses because the society we live in says they are acceptable ones, so why not tell lies to make your death more bearable to everyone but you . . . ?"

How quickly what was intended as a great, welcoming utopian construct devolves—under hypocrisy, economic pressure, sloth, and inefficiency—into a sprawling nightmare of exclusion, suffering, and inequity. We watch the local virtues that, moments ago, we were praising, transformed or unveiled as the manicheanisms that simply demand of us that we forget the suffering and pain of others if we are to effect the displacement and growth that was the initial motive for the movement from country to city, from small to big, from rural to urban (from low-density population to high-density population) in the first place. Can this be as true of churches or of schools as it can be of hospitals? Is it more or less likely to happen in schools supported by churches—such as the one Evenson taught at when he began this book? Is it more or less likely to happen in churches that have arranged supportive relations with the state?

Lots of history lie behind these questions. Sometimes it seems that history is nothing else but an attempt to answer them; and, under the pressures of weather, harvest, technology, and natural resources, different political decisions made to deal with their abuses mark the differences between freedom and oppression.

(One of the first facts of my language I remember learning as a child in the 1940s was that its longest legitimate word was "antidisestablishmentarianism." It meant to be against the separation of church and state. For at least a century now it seems to be—more and more—what we've suffered from. And the weather, crops, capital and banking interests, paper products manufacturers, oil interests, and transhumance a succession of political decisions try to respond to [or just the pig and chicken farms and privatized jails, along with attendant big pharma] have more and more to do with that shrinking separation, marked by things like the re-establishment of the death penalty, the defunding of Planned Parenthood, and the opposition to health care, not to mention opposition to the message of the current Pope himself.)

I repeat: *Father of Lies* is a horror novel. It is about both large institutional evils and about hidden personal horrors: and what happens when they meet. One sign of its intelligence, complexity, and nuance is that neither is presented as a simple, uncritical extension of the other. There is conflict between them. But there is support, too. It uses its genre to ask, what happens when those institutional evils come into conflict with evil that is well along into the hallucination and forgetfulness of individual psychosis?

In *Father of Lies* this conflict becomes the occasion for a set piece that gives us a kind of surreal trial—or rather a debate—between two parodic representations of Job-like proportions, the doctor, who is a stand-in for God, and the bloody-headed man, who takes the part of an ersatz Satan. (The writer of that initial faux Greek comedy concluded it with a happy ending that strikes many modern readers to be as inappropriate as that of *Huckleberry Finn* when Sawyer appears to take over at the end. Even so, we assume today we are supposed to read the debate in Job—and the positions of its debaters—seriously.) Evenson's is presented with the conviction of the most skillful narrative so that its surface seems more or less reliable: the difference however is that, in Job, not only Job but possibly Job-and-Satan as well exist in the mind of God. What does it mean, Evenson's novel asks us, when both God and Satan exist only in the mind of Job—who in this version exists as a psychotic murderer on the order of Easton Ellis's American Psycho, Patrick Bateman. What does all this mean about the social institution that gives Evenson's Fochs his power as well as access to the institutional margins in which he commits his atrocities. As well it impels the institution's final gesture. (I can't believe it's a serious spoiler: it is *the* anticipated ending of a certain kind of horror tale:) Fochs is displaced to another location where he will still be free to do what he does or even worse. Both the ending and the development toward it are entirely entailed with the moral warning for which we traditionally we read them.

But Evenson gives us something more—something to trouble that so familiar warning: Evenson's novel might quickly be described as turning on that single debate between devil and doctor. But he gives us several others—and they work to destabilize each other and the ends they lead to. One involves the compassionate therapist Feshtig, who is willing to challenge those above him in the institution in order to protect Fochs, until, with research, fieldwork, and careful inquiry, Feshtig can find out from Fochs's half brother, Myra, what is really going on. For me, this is one of the most powerful scenes in the book. In the Myra/Feshtig confrontation, about the nature of Fochs's childhood, we learn (one) it was probably the nightmare we might expect, if it was (two) not a good deal worse. But Myra gives us only fragments from which to extrapolate, and finally refuses to divulge "all." The coherent backstory we might expect from another kind of writer that would explain "all" is not forthcoming. Rather, Evenson gives us a far more realistic and believable portrait of Myra, in which we learn (three) he doesn't understand all of what happened to them as children himself, and (four) he feels a loyalty to what produced him and his insane half brother that he can see no reason to share with even the best intentioned stranger, such as Feshtig, who is so far from such a life there is (five) simply no way he *can* understand it. (From Feshtig's own diction and account of the meeting, I can understand that, even as Feshtig is the easiest character to identify with.) Myra has survived (or possibly not; or not as well as we might at first assume) what we expect and what Myra suggests *was* a nightmare for his half brother and only slightly less so for himself, much of it repressed on both their parts. The scene ends with the strongly implied understanding that Feshtig can either use what he has in a positive way if he can, or he can forget it. It's Feshtig's call. Myra has done what he can. Further details would only put more mud in water already unclear. A continuing irony, of course, is that while Feshtig—the closest the novel comes to a portrait of a traditionally "good man"—is trying futilely to get more information from Myra, Fochs is free to continue his enormities, whether committed on his family or in his community's night-alleys, jail cells, and hotel-hovels.

I point out here one other thing: for me the traditionally female name on the gruff male-appearing farmer and working-class half brother is the same order of sign for the unsettling of our sense of the culture he (and Fochs) hail from, which comes from the unknown insides of that culture, as the quote from Thiong'o that heads the book. Rather than the cliché reading you might give either (that is, what you already know about the way such signs are traditionally read in "our" culture), you might let both function as signs of what you do not know about the way they actually function in either culture (African or Mormon). That's how I prefer to read what Evenson is pointing to with both signifiers. To develop either reading responsibly, you would have to read more Thiong'o to find out what it meant. You would have to undertake a personal study of rural Utah culture even a born Mormon such as Feshtig (or Evenson) does not (or did not at the time) have access to.

Here is one of Evenson's most effective strategies. In many ways this is an anti-Stephen King horror novel: Evenson evokes what Hannah Arendt did in her 1960s coverage in that decade's *New Yorker* of the trials of the Nazi war criminal captured by Israel, Adolf Eichmann: the banality of evil. Rather than utilizing a Baudelairean or Paterian attempt to raid evil for the beauty it may contain or pick over the cascade of minute perceptions of the world in all its variety—evil or good—for what can enrich life, Evenson takes on the more austere task of comparing only the banality of evil (Fochs's over-quick description of the murder of a young girl out in the street one night; over-quick certainly because Fochs assumes the reader might find it too horrible to dwell on) with the banality of the everyday (an ordinary description of a bacon, egg, and cheese breakfast at the kitchen table with his family the next morning).

Neither Fochs nor his creator assumes that poetry—by which I mean the fine observation and intriguing juxtapositions in language about the social and material world, in terms of either—is the site where the reader might find redemption, as it would be, say, were it a Theodore Sturgeon tale: nor is it a tale in which the force of its prose in analyzing the horror down to its perceptual and psychological atoms, could, in its course, recombine according to whatever grammar might be useful in solving the social or psychological problems.*

---

*In Sturgeon's classic horror novella *Some of Your Blood,* the incredibly nice and quintessentially "normal" farm boy has ended up in the army brig either through a mistake or something so horrible it is beyond words to describe—at least in the discourse of 1957 popular fiction, when it first appeared. With further study, however, the boy doesn't seem quite so normal. He is an extreme loner, has shunned society all his adult life; and a string of unusual deaths of young women seem to have followed him since adolescence. What is *his* institutional (i.e., army) psychiatrist supposed to make of it . . . ?

Denouement of part I: this really nice kid who's had a really rough life does like to drink human blood—especially girls' and women's. But, practically, he doesn't need a lot, and he doesn't need it frequently. Not only that, he has several times tried to kill himself because of it. Denouement of part II: observation, knowledge, and specifics, even when they take us beyond the acceptable, will conquer all. Along with his general poverty, social and material, the kid has escaped anything like ordinary sex education—believable enough in the American rural fifties. Why doesn't he try asking his girlfriend for what he wants, and not as a bite on the neck or the wrist, but as a monthly favor consistent with female biology? At the end, this is all implied as discreetly as the evocations of rural life and social isolation are specific and luminous, so that, in effect, Sturgeon dares the reader not to buy it. Outside of a couple of mawkish pages of introduction, it's an astonishing performance.

Yes, it's awfully close to the mindless uplift we spoke of at the beginning. But isn't the simple verbal performance with its specificity, observation, and challenge of social commonplaces preferable, once the text gets underway, to the extravagant self-parody all this becomes under the regimes of *True Blood* and *Twilight* in the last decade? (Both of which, given the context of what else was available, I rather liked.)

If Evenson's work sits at the opposite pole from King's and Poe's, in his choice of story and structure, in his choice of verbal texture and narrative structure, it also sits at the opposite pole from Sturgeon's and Stephen Crane's. But the concert of all Evenson's choices, narrative and rhetorical, makes the book a serious—and sobering—story. Like much good horror, it's downright creepy; and, without a ghost in sight, it's haunting.

Wynnewood, October 25, 2015

Acknowledgments

I want to thank those who have shared their experiences with me in the course of writing this book—they have been invaluable in helping me understand the potential for abuse in religious hierarchies. Nevertheless, this is a work of fiction. It approaches a problem common in a wide range of religions. Any specific resemblance to actual persons or to any actual events is incidental.

Go home and observe these conditions. First, never tell anybody that you are a man without a soul. Second, when you reach home, seize the child you love most, pierce one of the veins in his neck, drink up all his blood until his body is completely dry, cook the body, eat the flesh.

Ngũgĩ wa Thiong'o, *Devil on the Cross*

FATHER OF LIES

Memorandum, Zion Foundation Institute of Psychoanalysis
From: Alexander Feshtig
To: Curtis Ballard Kennedy, Director

Director Kennedy:
I was somewhat surprised to receive your memorandum and even more surprised by your request. That you choose to contact me in such fashion rather than simply addressing me face to face suggests that you also see the request as problematic and are ashamed to make it. What you ask is a great deal more than an "imposition." It will necessitate in effect my compromising my commitments both at clinic and home so as to listen to the tapes again, put my notes in order, revise my initial draft, and draw what (necessarily fragmentary) conclusions I can manage. I am disinclined to do it.

When I initially accepted this position, I was assured by your predecessor that our clinic would be allowed to operate independently of the sponsoring religion, that I was to be guaranteed the same privacy and confidentiality in regard to doctor/patient relations which would be afforded me in private practice. Your memorandum, however, suggests that this is not now, and perhaps never has been, the case. We cannot be expected to operate effectively with the Church breathing down our necks; our clients must be guaranteed full confidentiality, and must have a safe environment in which to progress. In addition, there are legal issues at stake. If "the Church needs to know" the details of this case (which I doubt), I suggest that it contact Provost Fochs himself, seeking to gain his permission before approaching me.

I understand the difficulty of your position, but nothing will be gained from operating through secrecy and stealth. No matter how important or powerful or inspired the apostolic elder is who prodded you to make this request, it is a request that should not have been made. You have convinced yourself that if you do this single favor for him—if you violate your ethics on this one occasion—that that will be the end of it. But once he sees you are willing to operate in clandestine fashion, he will call upon you often. Patients will be directed toward the clinic specifically so that an elder of the Church will have ready access to their files.

Though apostolic elders are men of God, that does not make all they do (or that you do on their behalf) godly. They are human: they can, and will, make mistakes. Hell is crammed full of godly men.

Is this an official request of the institution or the private "suggestion" of one apostle of the Church? If it is an official request, I must insist it pass through official, public channels in the proper way. If it is an unofficial "suggestion," it must be ignored.

In short, I will not cooperate under such terms. I will not pass along to you my Fochs papers.

You have made a mistake in getting caught up in this. I can only wish you luck in extricating yourself as gracefully as possible.

Sincerely,
Feshtig

C. Ballard Kennedy, Director
Zion Foundation Institute of Psychoanalysis

Dear Elder Blanchard,

I was pleased to have your note, pleased as well to learn you hold my work in high regard. You are too kind. You are among the first to comment on the strengths of my article on Christian-based analysis—i.e. "Christianalysis"—though I hope you will not be the last. My present work continues along similar lines, postulating a psychoanalytic method which operates according to the inspired truths which our sacred books and our church leaders have revealed to us rather than according to the misunderstandings of worldly psychoanalysis and psychology. I believe it to be the sacred mission of all members of the Church to work actively to infuse their disciplines with the truth of the gospel, to shed the pure light of Christ over the shadowy professions of man.

In response to your query, I am sorry to say I know very little about the Fochs case. Dr. Alexander Feshtig has handled the case from beginning to end. Though it is clear that he is quite interested in the case, he has remained, as often is his wont, uncommunicative. He has declined to discuss the case or to make his tapes and notes available.

Since the request for information comes from an apostolic elder of the Church, I am willing to do as you ask. I think I will be able to gain access to at least some of Feshtig's notes and assorted papers on Fochs, though I would ask that you keep that between you and me. I would not normally do this: I have strict standards. But this is a special case. I know my duty to my profession but I know even better my duty as a member of the Church. I am certain you will handle the information I pass along in an inspired, cautious fashion.

By the way, I have a brother-in-law, a worthy and obedient member of the Church and a true scholar of the holy and revealed word of God, who has been adjunct faculty at our Church's university for a number of years. He has nearly been offered a full-time position several years running, but there are certain unchristian members of his department who refuse to recognize his merits, arguing that his work is not sufficiently rigorous. Yet, with his broad understanding of the inspired principles of the gospel, he is precisely the sort of teacher that would best serve the university! Is it too much of an imposition to ask if you have any advice as to how I might aid him to obtain the permanent position he deserves?

Sincerely,
Ballard Kennedy

C. Ballard Kennedy, Director
Zion Foundation Institute of Psychoanalysis

Dear Elder Blanchard,
Enclosed, as much as I could conveniently gather of Feshtig's anamnesis of Provost Fochs. My brother-in-law thanks you, and writes to say that he finds his new situation quite satisfying. I thank you as well for going to the trouble. You shouldn't have.

As far as I can determine, I have had access to a partial, preliminary case study. Anything further remains locked either in Feshtig's private cabinet, his house, or perhaps his briefcase. The work is characteristic Feshtig, far too secular in its conclusions.

I have not had access to his session tapes and have only managed to come by this portion of his work because Feshtig gave it to the secretary to type and she respects my authority. Feshtig is rather scrupulous about his current papers and tapes. I cannot gain access to them without arousing his suspicions.

I hope these papers will meet your needs. I am sorry I cannot give you more recent information.

Sincerely,
Ballard Kennedy

PART ONE

FIRST ANAMNESIS

Background

When I first met him, Eldon Fochs was a thirty-eight-year-old accountant as well as lay provost for the largely conservative religious sect the Corporation of the Blood of the Lamb ("Bloodites"). He was clean shaven, pale in complexion, respectably dressed in a fashion typical of the Church's leadership, wearing a dark, sturdy suit, a white shirt, and a conservative tie. In all our interviews, he never departed from this fashion of dress. He was a large, soft-spoken man, slightly overconscious of his body but nevertheless possessed of a relaxed demeanor. He had sought treatment at the request of his spouse, who was concerned by recent changes in his sleep behavior, which included "talking in his sleep in somebody else's voice," sleepwalking, and brief violent behavior toward his wife upon being awakened (behavior he had no memory of). Though Fochs believed his wife was overreacting, he chose to come to me nonetheless for two reasons: first to pacify her and second because during the past year he had had "disturbing dreams and thoughts" which he "wanted to be free of."

In our first interview, Fochs stated a preference for being called "Brother Fochs" or "Provost Fochs" or simply "Fochs" rather than being called by his first name, Eldon. He was initially reluctant to discuss his family history. The disturbing dreams and thoughts, he felt, had "nothing to do with the past" since they had only originated a year ago. When I persisted, however, I discovered that he was the eldest of two children, the youngest having died at birth. He "was brought up in the faith," growing up in a middle class Bloodite family in a predominantly Bloodite neighborhood. His earliest memories included his youngest brother's funeral, presided over by his father, a provost for the Church. He also remembered his mother helping him to learn to read out of the official Bloodite children's magazine, *Come Unto Me,* at age five, and the frequent absence of his father in his youth due to his church-related responsibilities.

Fochs remembered his mother as proper, loving, and industrious. She did not work outside of the home. She was very meek and often would look to her husband for advice even in simple household matters. The family had only one car, which Fochs's father took every day to work. His mother spent most of her time at home, except Wednesday afternoons when a neighbor would drive her to the grocery store. Nevertheless, the mother gave her son no sign of being discontent. Even when she lost her youngest child, leaving Fochs an only child, she told Fochs that it had been God's will and carried quietly on with her life.

He remembered his father as dignified, friendly, kind. His father was, Fochs indicated, most often absent in the evenings. The family understood the reasons for this and respected him for it, drawing strength from his "involvement with God." According to Fochs, the time his father did spend with the family was "quality time." His father "governed the household with kindness—sometimes sternly, but never with anger," administering punishment swiftly and without heat. Fochs sometimes thought of his father as being distant and withdrawn, but his mother explained this was because of the weight of his position in the Church. Both his father and mother are still alive and still happily married.

Family life as a whole was generally happy, and Fochs had had every advantage. He did not mind being an only child. He claimed he had always been introspective and preferred to have the majority of his time to himself.

The family began each day at 5:30 a.m. with family prayer and Bible study, directed by the father. Each day was ended with prayer and religious study as well, directed by the father unless he was absent, in which case Fochs, as the only other male (even though a child), took charge.

As a child, Fochs had had a frequently recurring dream. In the dream was a man whose head was all cut and bloody, who was asking him to do something—upon awakening, he could never remember what. In the dream he was never frightened, but upon awakening he was frightened. He claimed he had had this dream many times as a child.

When he was eleven, Fochs contracted pneumonia and grew very ill. His mother asked his father to give Fochs a blessing of healing, a practice typical in the Bloodite faith, but the father refused, saying the boy would heal on his own and that one shouldn't squander God's healing. Fochs did indeed recover, though he is now frequently subject to respiratory illness, perhaps as a result of the pneumonia. He claims not to blame his father for this, and says that his being alive today is proof that his father did not need to give the blessing.

As a teenager, Fochs had what he calls his "gray period." On a personal and private level, he stopped praying, stopped reading the Scriptures, and began to participate in activities that he describes now as "immoral," but whose exact nature he has been reluctant to specify. On a public level, however, he continued to attend church and to partake of Communion without confessing his sins. He did so because he didn't want others to suspect his shortcomings. Eventually the tension between what he was on Sunday and what he did during the week became too great. With some difficulty he changed his behavior and recommitted himself to the Church.

When Fochs was twenty-four, during his last year of college, he met the woman he would marry. One week later they became engaged, and six weeks after that he married her. He described his wife as having all the good qualities that a woman should have. Their first daughter was born ten months after their marriage, and since then they have had two sons (twins) and a daughter. Fochs says he is content with married life, and that although there are occasionally minor disagreements between himself and his wife, he is happy.

Pacifying His Wife

Fochs had come to visit me partly at his wife's request. He had recently begun to talk in his sleep, sometimes very loudly, often in a voice that was not his own. In a short note that Fochs handed to me in our first meeting, his wife described the voice as "sharp, biting, and full of malice," much different from Fochs's soft-spoken near-slur. She had heard his mouth speak like this three times. It spoke, she said, "using profane and pornographic language (language which my husband never uses while awake)" and seemed intent on recounting some sort of abusive, violent narrative, though Fochs's wife could not piece together more. The first time, she shook him and he stopped speaking. The second time, he began to wander through the house, apparently still asleep. She caught him as he was putting his coat on, preparing to go out the door. When she touched him and spoke to him, he (though still apparently asleep) allowed her to lead him back to bed. The third time, she had started to shake him but he continued speaking and then suddenly struck out at her. Fochs claimed he was asleep at the time, that he didn't know he was hitting anybody, that his body had struck her but that he had been "too deep inside myself to be responsible for the action."

Fochs has never been awake during his sleepwalking episodes. He seemed to want to minimize the importance of these and his other sleep disturbances.

Fochs's sleepwalking alone might be seen as a simple sleep disorder, but because of its combination with Fochs's talking in his sleep in a different voice and in different words than he would normally use, it deserves to be taken seriously as an indication of larger dissociative disturbance.

Paper

Fesh: I would like to try something a little different. Do you mind following along on something new?

Fochs: Sure.

Fesh: If I say to you, "Fochs, you're no longer a person, you're an object," what object first comes to mind?

Fochs: Well, I don't know. A slice [sic] of paper, I guess.

Fesh: What do you like about paper?

Fochs: It's flat. There's no thickness to it. You can only see one side at a time. But you always know the other side is there, and you can always turn it over and see the other side. Unless it's transparent paper. Then you can see both sides at once.

Fesh: Would you be opaque or transparent paper?

Fochs: Opaque.

Fesh: Would it be nice to be flat and have no thickness?

Fochs: You get rid of one dimension, down to two. Certainly, it simplifies things. But it's not a question of nice: it's just the way paper is. It can't help it.

Fesh: What needs to be simplified?

Fochs: I don't know, ask the paper.

Fesh: What wouldn't you like about being paper?

Fochs: What don't I like? I don't know, really. I can't think of anything. Paper is pretty much nothing but paper; everything it must be, nothing further.

Fesh: You can write on paper.

Fochs: Yes, and you can erase what is written.

Fesh: Unless it's written in pen.

Fochs: I always write in pen. Then you have to use white-out.

Fesh: What's written on the other side?

Fochs: What?

Fesh: If you're a piece of paper, what's written on your other side?

Fochs: How should I know? If it's on the other side, I can't see it, can I? Anyway, I'm not a piece of paper at all, am I.*

---

* Initially I believed the object-identification exercise's primary value had been as an exercise in self-identification and as an icebreaker. It raised issues that would surface again, most often in disguised form, in the later sessions—i.e., Fochs's sense of self-disconnection (two sides, one cannot see the other), his mistrust of interior experience (symbolized by his desire for a lack of interior space, a flatness without thickness), and his empirical conception of the self as largely created by external forces (writing on paper), a notion that the Church does not share.

The object-identification exercise also gave him a language with which to broach the subject of his disturbing thoughts.

Disturbing Thoughts

Once he was comfortable with me, Fochs himself raised the issue of his "disturbing thoughts." When I asked if he heard voices, he hesitated but said no, just "loud thoughts."

Fochs admitted these had to do with children.

"A child?"

"Lots of children."

"In what way?"

"In the thoughts, you might say it is as if I am writing on them."

"On them?"

"They have no clothing. I don't know what has become of their clothing."

"Writing on their skin?"

"Yes. My mouth is dry and I know it is wrong to do but I am doing it anyway."

"What are you writing?"

"Sometimes I am writing God's name. Most often I am writing my own."

He would at this time go no further. However, the suggestion was already present that these thoughts tended toward a pedophilic or pederastic nature, writing one's own name on the body of a child being as well a kind of indication or claim of ownership.

Fochs, on the grounds of the little he had told me, wanted me to "cure him." Yet he at first rejected my suggestion that if we were to go further, he would have to discuss the issue of the thoughts further and be honest about them. I told him that it was wrong to think if he arrested his thoughts on children, he would be cured. What was needed, I suggested, was a determination of what lay behind his thoughts, what had caused them to occur. Otherwise, though they might vanish momentarily, they would repeatedly resurface in different forms. He was somewhat impatient with this suggestion.

When I asked Fochs, in a later session, if he had thoughts written on his own body, he claimed there had been things written there, but he had erased them all. In the same session, he was finally willing to admit that the thoughts had been of a sexual nature, directed toward children.

"I would never act on such thoughts, mind you," he said. "I would never even tell people about them."

"You've told them to me."

"Sure," he said, smiling, "but you're not a person: you're a therapist."

Draw-a-Person (DAP Figures) Results

Fochs's first figure consisted of a profile of a head, small and to the lower left of the page. The head had a thick neck, a collar, and the beginnings of a tie. The figure was apparently male, simple and quickly done, but in bold strokes, the hair drawn as eight straight horizontal lines, as if blowing in a direction opposite of where the head faced. The mouth was a simple line which split the L-shaped angle of the front of the face and the chin. The lines of the face did not quite connect. The eye was lidless and incomplete. The tie and the shirt collar, however, were very carefully drawn. There was no shading, except for the knot of the tie, which was carefully darkened.

DAP interpreters have suggested that lack of body may be indicative of someone who has difficulty dealing with feelings or who favors the intellect over feeling. The care and detail used in drawing the collar and tie maximizes its importance in relation to the rest of the figure. The smallness of the figure and its placement low on the page can be read as an indication of insecurity. That the figure was drawn looking to the side rather than straight ahead might be indicative of Fochs self-identifying with this picture less than with the picture that follows.

The second figure Fochs drew was a complete body, filling the entire page, looking directly forward, one eye higher than the other. The eyes and the nose were the only clear portions of the figure. The mouth was extremely distorted. There seemed to be no clothing or shoes. The figure itself was a mess of scrawled and overlapped lines, the body not clearly male or female, hands and feet undifferentiated, the boundaries of the figure fluid and made by suggestion from the disjoined scrawls rather than clearly delineated, the figure gapped and porous.

This second figure is perhaps most significantly interpreted in relation to the first drawing. In the first drawing, Fochs used bold strokes and lines to draw the head of the figure, yet all these terminated in the carefully drawn collar and tie. This might be read as symbolizing the way in which Fochs is controlled by his Church. The second figure, on the other hand, had broken out of that control, had a fuzziness that might be seen as representing freedom—it was not even clear that it was wearing clothing—and perhaps was Fochs's wish-fulfillment representation of himself.

When I asked him about the sex of the figures, he indicated both were male, despite the fact that in asking him to draw a second figure I had requested he draw a person of a gender different from the first drawing's figure. His fixation on males is perhaps due to his acceptance of the rigid and traditional gender roles taught by the Bloodite faith, which leads often to a devaluation of women.

"Which figure do you like better?"

He pointed to the second figure.

"Why?"

"It's a better drawing. It's more artistic."

"What else do you like about it?"

"That it's drawn better."

"What does it make you think of?"

"It reminds me of someone in my dream."

Religious Inadequacy

Fochs had feelings of inadequacy and worthlessness, resulting at least in part from his church-related duties as a provost. Indeed, both his sleep disturbance and his disturbing thoughts and dreams did not begin until shortly after he was asked to be the provost.

As he became more comfortable with me, he expressed his doubts about his role in the Church. He declared to me that he was "not worthy," that he "had been called to serve as provost against God's better judgment," that "God had allowed the Church to make a mistake." We discussed whether he had any legitimate grounds to feel unworthy, but from the information he gave me, it seemed that he was more committed and faithful than most members of the Church. Indeed, perhaps too committed: he would feel guilty if he went a day without reading in his Scriptures or if he missed a prayer. He had maintained an idealized view of church leaders, believing them to be more than mortal. He, in his own mind, didn't meet the ideal. There were the "thoughts on children" as well, as he had taken to calling them. He was convinced that "sins of thought" were nearly as bad as sins of action, and that it was a short distance from one to another.

In the course of his therapy, I tried to work against Fochs's hypersensitivity and his delusion-based guilt and lead him to a more productive understanding of his relation to himself and to the Church. Fochs's guilt about religious issues seemed tied to his father's strong commitment to the Church, and the sense that Fochs's father and mother both perhaps unconsciously gave him that religion should come before all else. Indeed, Fochs's strongest memories of his father were related to his father's involvement in the Church.

As a youth, Fochs was made to believe that only the most worthy men would be asked to be provosts. He had his father held up to him constantly as an example of someone who lived an ideal life, and he not only looked up to his father but saw him as perfect. He never moved beyond an idealized image of his father. He had frequently worried that he would not measure up, but had gradually suppressed these fears. However, his anxiety was reawakened when he found himself in the church position he associated with his father (when he found himself in essence playing his father's role), in his father's place as a provost but still human, with flaws and faults, and with thoughts that he believed his father never could have had. Since all worthy Bloodite males receive some form of the priesthood, and since a great emphasis is placed on exercising one's priesthood worthily, uncertainty about one's priesthood or one's role in the Church may precipitate doubts about personal identity.

Fochs was extremely reluctant to trace his difficulties back to the archaic idealized image of his father that he had objectified and internalized as a child. He continued to insist on the accuracy of that internalized object, proved unwilling to acknowledge his father as a real external being, as a nonidealized person with faults and flaws. He continued to insist that his father had been perfect.

Fochs vs. Provost

Fochs liked to think of his difficulties as originating at the moment he was called to be provost over a sizable congregation. He claimed to have had no feelings of unworthiness until this time, though everything he revealed about his personal history and all he admitted to me about his relationship with his parents, his father in particular, suggested that a sense of inadequacy had been firmly entrenched early in life. His being asked to be a provost merely brought to the surface what he had been troubled by most of his life. Yet despite all evidence to the contrary, Fochs repeatedly insisted he had had "high self-esteem" until he became a provost. He said he shouldn't have been assigned to be provost. He believed the area rector who presided over the local area had given him the assignment not because of his merits but because he wanted something done and knew Fochs would do it.

In the interview in which the assignment of provost was extended, the area rector asked Fochs no questions about his moral worthiness and Fochs volunteered nothing about himself. The area rector told Fochs that he needed someone who would be completely obedient, and when Fochs expressed his willingness to be so, he extended the assignment to him. Paradoxically, because the area rector did not question him about his moral worthiness, Fochs saw this as evidence that he *must* be unworthy. Since the area rector also talked a great deal about a woman in Fochs's congregation whom he said must be excommunicated, Fochs believed he had been made provost largely because the area rector knew he would follow orders and excommunicate the woman. The current provost had refused to excommunicate her. He "didn't know his duty," the area rector told him. The area rector knew, he said, that Fochs would "follow orders."

The individual in question was a mother of six, a faithful and involved member of the Church. The area rector wanted her excommunicated because she had publicly written what Fochs called "the unthinkable opinion" that the Holy Spirit, the third member of the Godhead, might be female.

"You didn't want to excommunicate her?" I asked.

"But I did," he said. "This woman was a heretic."

"How did you know she was a heretic?"

"The area rector told me she was."

"What made you believe him?"

"He was a man of God. He was the area rector, and he was speaking in his official capacity as a church leader," Fochs said. "And an apostolic elder told him. Of course I believed him."

Fochs believed that church authorities would never lead him astray. He believed that whatever a church leader says, speaking in his official capacity, was new scripture and must be immediately obeyed. Even if a church leader were to ask him to do something "contrary to decency," he would be blessed for following him and doing it, *even if he knew it was wrong.*

Yet, at the same time, Fochs had convinced himself that he had been assigned to a position that he was hardly worthy to hold. He had accepted the position of provost because he thought it was better to be obedient than to question the area rector's decision and also because he was sure that God needed him to excommunicate the "heretic." He convinced himself that as soon as the woman was excommunicated and his task was done, someone else would be put in his place.

But after the woman was excommunicated, they did not release him. He found himself in a difficult position: his awareness of himself and his own flaws would not fit the image of church leaders that he had idealized. Either he had to believe that he was unworthy and had been called in error (which would mean severely questioning the infallibility of his leaders) or he had to believe he was worthy, despite the reservations he had about himself because of the archaic idealized image of his religious father.

Faced with this dilemma, Fochs chose to believe both. On the one hand, as a provost, he saw himself as worthy, but he was unable to justify in this context the thoughts he seemed to be having as Fochs. As Fochs, he was guilty. As provost, he remained innocent. The result was a partitioning of the self, which was manifested through disturbing thoughts, through sleepwalking, through speaking in an odd voice while asleep, and through his "disturbing dreams."

Provisional Diagnosis

DSM-IV criteria related to Dissociative Identity Disorder (DSM-III, Multiple Personality) were not met by Fochs, though when I asked Fochs if he ever felt like there was another person with a different name inside of him, he hesitated for some time. Instead of looking at me, he seemed to be looking past me. Then he responded:

"Inside of me? With a name?"

"Yes," I said.

"No, there's nobody like that inside me."

"Have you ever had any kind of supernatural experience?"

"Supernatural, no. I've had a lot of religious experiences."

"What sorts of religious experiences?"

"Faith-promoting experiences. Sometimes I can feel Christ so strong it's almost like he's present."

"Have you ever felt possessed?"

"Possessed? By a demon?"

"Or by someone else, either good or bad."

"Sometimes I let Jesus take charge."

"What happens when Jesus takes charge?"

"Maybe take charge isn't the right phrase. Sometimes I have these thoughts. When I have them, I just feel that I know what Christ wants me to do, so I do it."

"What kinds of things?"

"Just things."

"What sorts of things?"

"Nothing special, really. Just everyday things."

"Are these thoughts voices?"

"No. Just loud thoughts."

Because of the Bloodite belief in the possibility of personal communion with God, these beliefs were not alarming or unusual in and of themselves. Interesting, though, was Fochs resorting to approximate answers to avoid specifying the thoughts. His sense of hearing and knowing what Christ wants, his sleep disorders, and his feelings of worthlessness, all seem to be tied to his sense of himself in relation to the Church on one hand and to his father as a church leader on the other hand (the first symptom as a desire to be led in his duty as a church leader, the second symptom as a kind of reaction to his church duty—the expression of a long-denied aspect of his personality—the third symptom as again an acknowledgment of the gap between himself as a person and his formalized idea of what a provost is and what his father was).

With this in mind, I made a provisional diagnosis of Dissociative Order NOS, with Axis II: Parasomnia.

Pecking Order

Fochs's internal fissure found means of expression and consequently solidification when Fochs was "encouraged" to excommunicate the heretic. Indeed, in our conversations, it became clear that despite his religious reservations about her, he empathized with her in a way that made it almost seem for him that he occupied both sides of the church court, that he was both the "Judge in Zion" and the sinner to be cast out (Provost vs. Fochs).

For Fochs, the woman was a means of expressing what he had repressed—a catalyst his mind used to perform its operations. It was clear from how he spoke about her that he hardly considered her to be a person in her own right. His actions in her church court (at least as he reported them to me) seem to suggest this: more than anything else he seems to have been prosecuting himself, trying in essence, by excommunicating her, to excise what were the negative parts of his soul. The woman, the reality of her suffering, were neither acknowledged nor understood.

Despite his surface kindness and civil demeanor, Fochs seems to acknowledge people only rarely as people *per se*—more often they are counters in a patriarchal system, to be recognized by their titles, by their rank in the Church. Fochs is the same way with his family, referring most often in our sessions to his wife as "my wife" and his daughters as "my youngest" and "my eldest." Only his boys, the twins, are consistently referred to by Fochs by name, perhaps because they, as males, will one day hold the priesthood.

In this Fochs seems to have accepted to the fullest degree the patriarchal order that often becomes confused with the Church's gospel. Men for him are real, while the value of women seems to come in their subsidiary relationship to men—women for men like Fochs are not people: they are wives, mothers, daughters.

The Thoughts on Children

Having Fochs fully acknowledge and discuss his "thoughts on children" was critical to effective analysis and treatment, but it took some time before he would speak about these thoughts in anything but vague metaphors. As I had suspected, they involved abuse of children. The thoughts, he claimed, he couldn't stop or control, though once he had thought one he'd be "left alone" for a little while.

> I can be just walking down the street and see a young child, you know, eleven or twelve, walking home from school carrying schoolbooks. I won't think anything about it. But in a block the child is still in my head and without clothing now, and in another block I am doing things to the child's body, and in another block . . . [a long silence]. It's hard for me to talk about this. In another block the child is battered and beaten and dead.
>
> Then another block and it's over. I'm fine again. Just like normal. I go on with my day.

Such thoughts, Fochs claimed, were always threatening to assert themselves not as thoughts but as reality. It was wrong for him to think them, he felt, but he could not stop. And if Fochs imagined himself engaged in an act of sexual violence, he would remember it vividly and suffer guilt over it as if he had actually committed it.

Fochs's thoughts about children seemed related to his sleep disorders and to his difficulties with his church position. They were a means of reasserting himself in the face of doubt, allowing him to imagine himself in a position of power. During the thoughts themselves and for a short period thereafter, he felt above and beyond guilt. Yet, soon, because he doubted his worthiness to be a church leader and because he felt that the thoughts were wrong, he was nearly incapacitated by guilt. His life thus became inscribed into a vicious circle, in which the tension of guilt would lead to thoughts of a deviant nature and momentary release, followed by a period of rest and the subsequent return of guilt, the cycle moving more and more rapidly. His sleep behavior (parasomnia) can be seen as providing a similar sort of release.

Sex

I asked Fochs if as a child he had ever been approached for sex by another child or by an adult.

"I don't remember," he said. Later, he stated that had he been approached or even accepted (which, he insisted, he would never have done), it wouldn't have mattered. He had been washed clean when he had been baptized at age twelve and anything that came before that had never happened.

"Anyway," he said, "nothing like that ever really happened to me. And even if it had happened, God would have washed it away."

A Dream of Boys

From the first, Fochs attempted to be a model provost. He conducted worthiness examinations every six months with each of the youth of his congregation, as recommended by the official Bloodite *Provost's Handbook of Private Instructions.* He asked me in his early sessions if it was a good idea for him to meet with the youth, considering the thoughts he was having about children. Wasn't it possible, he asked, that such thoughts might translate into action? At the time I felt that to work productively to help the youth might force Fochs to see them as people, and thus give him encouragement to face his thoughts on children and learn to control them. I encouraged him to continue meeting with the youth as usual, but we agreed that if at any moment he became too uncomfortable, he should suspend the interview and telephone me.

The interviews seemed to move forward without problems. Soon after beginning them, however, Fochs admitted that he had begun to have dreams about some of the specific youth in his congregation. These dreams felt so real he wasn't always immediately certain they were dreams—on first awakening, they felt more like harrowing memories. He said that his fear that the dream might somehow be real (or if it wasn't real, his fear that it might *become* real) had made him reluctant to meet with the youth.

In the dream there was a boy, about twelve years old. Fochs called him into his office to speak of initiating him into the priesthood. In interviewing him, he asked the boy if there was anything he had done that would make him "unworthy to accept the gift of the priesthood." The boy shuffled his feet and mumbled no, but Fochs said that he could tell from the way the boy rested his hands one over the other that he wasn't telling the truth. Fochs felt a peculiar sense of disquiet, and this disquiet he felt literalized in his own breath, which gathered into a figure beside him. The dream went through a phase shift and the shaped breath configured into human form.

This man made of breath insisted that Fochs continue to prod the boy until he confessed. It would be better for the boy to get it off his mind, the man told him. If it hadn't been for this man, Fochs claimed, he would have let the boy alone.

I asked him to describe what the man made of breath looked like once he had solidified. He said the man was wearing tattered clothing and had a "shaved, razor-knicked head." I asked him what the man's name was. He said that he did not know but he did not think he had a name.

Fochs asked the boy again if there was anything he wanted to confess. The boy shook his head emphatically.

Fochs came out of his chair, feeling a little more urgent and distraught, and took a chair next to the boy. He took the boy's hand in his own hand, though the boy resisted slightly. When the man of breath began to prod him again, Fochs repeated the question, staring without blinking into the boy's face. The boy seemed frightened, and this, Fochs believed in the dream, was fear because of his guilt rather than fear of the sudden shift in Fochs's behavior.

The room grew darker and smaller. The other man dissolved into breath and was "drawn back in." Fochs and the boy were left alone.

"Why are you lying?" he asked the boy.

The boy glanced toward where the door had been. The door was not there anymore. Fochs said he could feel the boy's panic, and in the dream he liked the way it felt. The boy pulled his legs up into the chair and hid behind his knees.

"The boy insisted he wasn't lying," but Fochs said God told him that the boy was lying.

He grabbed the boy's mouth, opened it and tried to look in, stretching the jaws apart until the boy began to cry, his tonsils throbbing. Fochs saw his crying as an admission of guilt. He let go and told the boy that God loved him and that he loved him as well. All he wanted, he said, was to help.

He forcibly took the boy's hand again and asked for the truth. He told the boy he needed to know what happened. He needed to know the details. The boy was sobbing now, rubbing his arms, but still insisted there was nothing to tell.

"I don't think you even know what truth is," Fochs remembered saying. "I think you need me to force the truth out of you."

"No," said the boy. "I told the truth."

"I know what you need," Fochs said. "Don't tell me I don't know."

He said he told the boy to turn to face the wall. At that point he was inspired by God "to know the boy's sin and to understand it thoroughly." The "sin" was that the boy had been sexually abused by an uncle and that he had sinned by not resisting the abuse sufficiently.** The boy, frantic, terrified, denied everything.

> God told me that where evil had made its mark, good must follow, burning evil out and purifying the body. I told the boy to remove his pants and he eventually shucked them. I told the boy to remove his underwear and when he would not I stripped those down myself. I could feel God endowing me with holy power. I reminded the boy that I was his spiritual leader and that obedience was the law upon which all other laws were predicated. If he didn't listen to what I said and obey me, he would go to hell. Not to hell, I said, but to the nothingness beyond hell, which would make hell look like a picnic. Then I told him to reach down and grab his ankles but to keep his legs as straight as he could. But he wouldn't

** Blaming the victim is common practice among Bloodite clergy.

> do it, so I had to do it for him. I came up behind him and held my hand over his mouth, wrapping the other around his chest. Then where evil had been before I forced good in until he bled.
>
> I told him I was going to have to keep cleansing him until all the evil was worn out and until he would admit his uncle had violated him. He said he didn't have an uncle. But everybody has an uncle. Everybody has an uncle, don't they?
>
> He kept falling down. I kept it up for awhile until I thought the evil was probably gone and then asked him, "Do you admit it?" and he said, crying, "Yes, I admit it!"
>
> So I had been right all along. God had not misled me. I told him I was proud of him for telling the truth and then helped him to dress.

Fochs spoke seriously with the boy. He told the boy that the Lord God commanded him to be silent about this. "Not that what we did here was secret," Fochs said, "but sacred." He told the boy that all Bloodites did the same. He told the boy that if he told anyone, God would pluck out his tongue and "it would never return, not even in the afterlife."

Each time he had the dream, Fochs said, he woke up highly disturbed and wrote down all he could remember. By the time he told me about the dream, he had formalized it, made it into a coherent narrative which, he admitted, was actually several versions of the dream pasted together.

There was also, sometimes, and with more and more frequency, a second sequence to the dream.

He was alone in his office, the first boy having left, when suddenly he felt he should open the door. He found a second boy in the hall, confused, nervous, reluctant to enter. Fochs brought him in and without the preliminaries of an interview told the boy he had to force the evil out and summarily raped him.

"But I should have waited for God's holy blessing," he said. "I should have waited."

He was alone in the dark, the boy gone, a voice telling him what he had done had been wrong, that the evil must be confessed before it can be expelled. Now, the voice said, Fochs had done evil, and he must be punished.

He could not identify the voice.

He could hear a sound, which he knew was of a man unbuckling his belt.

He awoke in a state of extreme anxiety.

Dream of the Murdered Girl

As with his other recurring dream, Fochs expressed fear, because of the vividness of the dream, that it was either based on a memory of an actual event or was something he could conceivably do in the future.

As we discussed the dream, it became clear that the girl described in the dream was based on a real girl, a member of his congregation who actually had been found murdered a few months prior, not long before our first meeting.

Fochs claimed to have been influenced by the same person as in the other dream, the figure of breath become flesh, but in this case the person was not separate from him but was grafted onto Fochs himself as a second head that only he could see. The head had claimed that the only way to save the girl was to kill her. Fochs, against his will, found his body compelled to do so.

The figure of breath was again without name. In the dream's first manifestations, Fochs strangled the girl with his own hands and then subsequently dismembered her. In its later occurrences, the dream shifted away from the act of murder and toward discovery of the dead girl. Fochs was no longer the killer, but rather the person who stumbled onto the body:

Fochs: I had a dream about the girl last night. I was out looking for her. It was as if I were awake and seeing it as it actually happened.

Fesh: What girl do you mean?

Fochs: The dead one. She was in the woods, kneeling at a stone altar, praying. The crown of her head was shiny. When I came closer I could see she was not moving. I reached out and touched her head and felt that the shine was oil. As soon as I touched her, I knew she was dead.

Fesh: What did you do then?

Fochs: I looked at her and looked away. When I looked again I could no longer see her head.

Fesh: Her head was gone?

Fochs: I couldn't see her head. I was worried for her.

Fesh: Why were you worried for her?

Fochs: Wouldn't you be worried for somebody if their head came up missing?

Fesh: But she was already dead, wasn't she?

Fochs: Yes, but not having a head seems worse. I mean, if you don't have it, somebody else must have it, right? And who knows how they're planning to use it?

That's what I thought in the dream anyway. The next thing I knew I was down on my hands and knees crawling around. After a while I realized I was looking for the head.

Fesh: Did you find it?

Fochs: She was still wearing it but she had twisted it backward and was hiding it behind her, between her shoulder blades. That way she could look backwards.

Fesh: Why would she want to look backwards?

Fochs: Maybe she was afraid someone was going to try to sneak up behind her. She was right to be afraid of that. I remember telling myself that she should have had two heads, one to watch in front of her as well.

Fesh: Did you have two heads?

Fochs: In the dream I did.

In actuality, the murdered girl's head had been twisted to a position identical to that which Fochs's dream had described. I do not believe this information was available at the time Fochs told me his dream, though I may be wrong. His other descriptions were similarly vivid but, for the most part, nothing he could not have gathered from reading the newspapers.

The mind uses the material available to it and reforms it to satisfy its own needs. In addition to scene changes and time gaps, there were always details in his dreams that did not correspond to the newspapers, the most notable of these being a piece of paper Fochs dreamed had been placed under the girl's tongue:

Fesh: Did you see who placed it there?
Fochs: No.
Fesh: Did you place it there yourself?
Fochs: God told me to put it there, but I have no memory of doing so.
Fesh: You put it there?
Fochs: It was a piece of paper. Something written on it. A *B* and an *H*.
Fesh: What do you think the letters referred to?
Fochs: I don't know. I didn't choose them—God did.

Because Fochs was the provost of a congregation, I believed he felt responsible when something serious happened to one of his members. Since Christ in the Bible has the shepherd leave the ninety-and-nine to go search for the one lost sheep, Fochs felt that he should have done the same. He was blaming himself for not having prevented the girl's death, playing this guilt out in his dreams.

Fesh: How could you have prevented the murder?
Fochs: I don't know. I could have been there for her. I could have known something was wrong.
Fesh: You couldn't have known someone was going to kill her. You were her provost. You were helping her as best you could.
Fochs: Yes, but maybe if I had said just the right thing . . .

Fesh: The only person who should feel responsible for the murder is the person who killed her. Can you believe that?

Fochs: I want to believe that.

In Place of a Conclusion

I have reached an end of the information currently available to me. Before drawing anything but tentative conclusions, however, I want to know more about Fochs. Since Fochs suddenly broke off his interactions with me at what I felt was the most productive stage, the analysis feels incomplete.

Fochs strikes one initially as a well-ordered, well-adjusted man. Yet looking back over my notes and listening to the tapes again, I am surprised to find that statements he made that originally felt convincing to me now feel disingenuous. Fochs is a more complex study than he initially appeared.

Fochs seems able to function in society, though it is clear his sleep disorder is part of a condition both deep rooted and quite complex.

I remain convinced, for the moment, that Fochs is suffering primarily from Dissociative Disorder NOS. However, there are enough other symptoms to suggest other possibilities, and thus I believe this to be only a partial diagnosis.

I am convinced as well that at least a few, though far from all, of the symptoms Fochs has described to me are factitious, and that he has on occasion been purposefully deceptive.

PART TWO

MAN OF GOD

CHAPTER 1

Blessing

Near evening the girl passes the house again, this time looking distraught. I watch her walk before the front window, slowly, swaying her slight hips. The salad tongs are motionless and caught in my hands.

She disappears beyond the hedge.

At the other end of the table, my youngest daughter is refusing to eat. My wife attempts to interest her in bits of chicken, eventually resorting to pushing them between the girl's teeth. My daughter keeps her lips closed. My wife begins to threaten, my daughter to cry.

I quickly finish my plate, then pull my youngest from her high chair. I take her to the sink, splashing water on her face and hands. Removing her bib, I dry her face with the reverse of it, then lower her to the floor. She takes a few awkward steps along the side of the cabinet, then lets go, staggers out of the room.

"She'll never learn to eat if you keep doing that," my wife says. "You spoil her."

"Be gentle with her," I say. "Give her time."

The girl outside is still transfixed in my head, the ghost of her still passing the window. She was distraught, I tell myself, or so she appeared. Perhaps she is in need of a little spiritual counsel. It is my duty to care for my flock, to look after the sheep, to give my life fully over to them and to the Lord. I should, the Holy Spirit tells me, seek her out to offer her comfort. But I can hardly just leave, can I? What would my wife think?

And then the Lord shows me the way.

I go into my study and close the door behind me. I dial the number for my congregation's volunteer secretary.

"Allen," I say. "Provost here."

"The provost?" he says. "What's wrong?"

"Provost here," I say. "Why would anything be wrong? Just a little question for you."

"Shoot," he says.

I bang the telephone against the tabletop.

"Allen?" I say at some distance from the receiver. "Allen? Are you there?"

"What?" he says. I can hear his voice perfectly. "What's wrong?" he asks.

"Can you hear me, Allen?" I ask. "Are you still there?"

"I'm here," he says. "Can't you hear me?"

"Something must be wrong with the line. I've been having trouble with this telephone all day. I am going to hang up. If you are hearing this, call me back. Call me back immediately."

I hang up the telephone. Waiting, I stare at my reflection in the handpiece's white plastic until the telephone begins to ring. I let it ring twice, to be sure my wife hears it, but snatch it up before my wife can think to pick up the extension.

"Hello?"

"It's Allen," he says. "Can you hear me now?"

"Yes," I say. "I can hear you perfectly."

"What was wrong?"

"Just one of those things," I say.

"You should have the line looked at," he says. "Well, what can I do for you?"

I invent something on the spur of the moment, pretending I have lost the schedule of Sunday's church interviews. He rummages out a copy from his file and reads the list to me. I pretend to write the names and times of the appointments down, then, thanking him, hang up the telephone.

"Who just called?" my wife asks when I step out of the den.

"Allen," I say. "Something has come up. I'll have to go over to the church building for a few hours."

"Tonight?" she asks. "Can't it wait?"

"Tonight. Emergency. Can't be helped."

"Take the baby out of the bath before you go," she says.

"I wish I could," I say. "But this one is urgent." I come close to her and embrace her, kiss her damp forehead. "I'm late as it is. I'll make it up to you, honey," I say. "Promise."

I see her again just as she passes into the trees, her white shirt aglow in the near dark. Parking the car a block from the path, I walk quickly to the guardrail and slip over it, splashing across the creek, shallow now for late summer, and cut across through Max Barton's field. Pushing through the rows of corn, I ease over the barbed wire backing the field, slip into the woods beyond.

The woods are denser than I expect, the sight of the field soon lost. The aspen have grown close together, the bark peeling into paper-thin curls, bushes and undergrowth between the trees. I push in, branches and leaves cracking like bones beneath my feet.

I come through the bushes into a clearing to find the girl there, facing the other way, sitting on a large rock with ungodly phrases spray painted all over it. She is scratching at the dirt with a stick. She has been weeping, I see, her makeup streaked with tears, her eyes gone thick and black around the rims where the mascara is melted and smeary.

"Is anything the matter?" I ask.

She startles, springs up and looks around. I come slowly forward through the bushes so that she can see the whole of me, my face too.

"What are you doing here?" she asks.

"Don't you know who I am?"

"Of course I know who you are," she says. "I see you every Sunday."

"I am glad you know who I am," I say. "I didn't think you knew."

"I do," she says.

"Why haven't you ever introduced yourself? Why have you never made an appointment to see me?"

She scratches in the dirt a little. "I thought you were busy," she says. "I didn't want to bother you."

"It's no bother," I say. "I feel I should get to know all the young people in my congregation. They're the future of the Church. The young people are the ones who need me most."

I step a little farther into the clearing, leaning my back against the bole of a tree while motioning for her to sit on the rock. She looks briefly over but remains standing.

"How did you know I was here?" she asks.

"You've been crying, haven't you?"

She looks down, twists her hands up. It is hardly an attractive pose.

"Do you want to talk about it?"

"No," she says.

"That's what a provost is for. To talk things over. To let you talk your problems through. To give you relief."

She doesn't say anything. But she hasn't run yet. She is as good as mine.

"Do you want to know why I came here? Shall I tell you what brought me?" I ask.

"I don't know," she says.

"It was the Lord. I was prompted. He told me that I should come. I didn't know why, so I tried to ignore the feeling, but the prompting kept coming. So I listened and came. You know why the Lord wanted me to come out here?"

"Why?" she says.

"For you," I say.

She ducks her head, cannot seem to look me in the eyes.

"I mean it. God loves you. He wants to help you. He wants you to tell me why you've been crying."

"No," she says. "I can't."

"I've heard every kind of sin. Nothing you say can surprise me. Nothing you say can shock me or make God love you less. You can tell me anything," I say, smiling. "I know sin inside and out."

I make my way a little farther into the clearing.

"I won't tell your parents. It will be just between you and me and God."

I stand and walk slowly toward her, trying to appear relaxed, approaching her casually.

"You can trust me," I say. "If you can't trust the Lord's anointed, who can you trust?"

I am close enough that I am able to reach out, touch her arm. She recoils, begins to recoil anyway. Then relaxes. She lets me lead her by the hand to the rock and seat her there. I kneel before her, holding her hands and staring up into her face. I imagine it makes quite a tableau.

"Tell me."

She shudders, starts to cry again. I lean forward and put my arms around her. Her body feels warm.

"That's right. Cry it out."

I hold her, smelling her hair, the faint damp odor of her nose as it runs sticky onto my shoulder.

"Do you feel better now?"

Shaking her head, she pulls herself slowly away.

"I just want to help you," I say. "You have to trust me."

She nods.

"Is it hard to talk about?"

She nods again, her face contorting, a red-blotched and twisting creature pushing through to the surface of her skin, her young beauty sloughed momentarily off.

"Do you trust me?"

"Yes," she says. "I guess so."

"Whatever you did, I am not going to think any less of you for it. We all make mistakes. It's only when we don't repent of our mistakes that we end up in trouble."

"I can't say it!" she bawls. "I can't talk about it!"

I am losing patience. She is not proving herself the girl her figure promises each night in the way she walks past my house.

"Shall I try to guess?"

She nods.

"You sinned alone?"

She shakes her head.

"With another person?"

Nods.

"Was there a third person involved? Just the two of you? Stole something?"

She doesn't answer.

"Killed someone?"

She shakes her head.

"Fornicated?"

She hesitates, nods, keeps nodding, starts weeping. My mouth goes dry, my tongue cleaving to the roof of it. The surface of my skin comes everywhere alive.

"It is not the end of the world," I say. "There are worse things you could have done." I draw myself a little closer to her, put my hand delicately on her arm. "God needs to know all the details. That is his way. I want to know everything."

I wait but she won't speak.

"You fornicated with someone your own age?"

"Yes," she says, her voice barely audible.

"He forced you, didn't he?"

She hesitates. Then shakes her head no.

"He must have forced you. I know boys. He was probably smooth enough to make you think otherwise, but he forced you."

She barely nods, just willing to acquiesce.

"How many times? Two or three?"

"More," she says.

"More? How often? Hundreds? Did you use birth control?" I let my hand stroke her arm. "Did he?"

She shakes her head.

"Did you think it would be less of a sin if you didn't?"

"I don't know," she says, and starts crying again.

"You don't know?"

She closes her eyes, covers her face with her hands.

"You're pregnant."

She says nothing, just stays with her face covered. So I figure I am right.

"God is telling me you are," I say.

She nods her head slowly.

"That's hard, very hard, but there are worse things that could have happened to you. It isn't the end of the world." I move my hand to touch her neck. "Some punk kid did it, I guess."

"No," she says. "Not just someone."

"You met him at high school?"

She doesn't say anything, doesn't move.

"Don't tell me you met him at church?"

I look around slowly, then back to her. It is nearly dark now, difficult to see.

"How long have you known him?"

In a low, quavery voice she manages, "A long time."

"Old family friend, is he?"

She shakes her head.

"Do you think this is some sort of game?" I say. "Can't you just tell me the truth?"

She doesn't say, just sits with her head cupped in her hands. I stroke her hair.

"You can't run from it. You need to turn and face it."

Then suddenly I figure it out. I withdraw my hand.

"Your brother?" I say.

"Is it?" I say.

"Is it?" I say, shaking her.

At first she shakes her head but then starts to nod, or her head nods itself as I shake her, her teeth rattling as she tries to cry out. I let go of her and she falls backwards off the rock. She starts to scramble backwards, and I scramble backwards as well, until the two of us are crouched at either side of the clearing, staring at each other, our bodies dissolving into the darkness. I expect her to push her way into the trees and vanish but she stays where she is, poised, unwilling to step back out of the clearing.

"Don't worry," I say, though I do not believe it. "There is nothing to worry about. It is out now, isn't it? You must feel better for having told me."

She neither moves nor speaks, stays crouched and panting, her breath coming out ragged, like an animal's.

"There's a place awaiting you in hell, but you don't have to go," I say. "I can help you repent. God loves you. If you do as I say, he will save you."

I begin to crawl across the clearing, toward her, on my hands and knees. She stays fixed, perhaps not fully aware of my approach. I feel the ground damp on my knees through my slacks.

"God wants to embrace you. He wants to reveal to you his love."

She lets me come closer but before I can embrace her she begins to edge free of the clearing. I stand.

"You don't want to disappoint God. You've already betrayed him enough. You had better stay right where you are and listen to me while you have the chance."

I get her by the hands and pull her up against me. She struggles a bit, then stops, goes listless. Probably the same way she acts with her brother, I bet.

"There now," I say. "Doesn't that feel better?"

I fumble at her clothing a little bit, nothing really, and she starts striking my chest. I let go of her, she steps back off balance over the rock, falls, begins to scramble backwards again.

"Obedience is the law on which all other blessings are predicated," I call to her. "There is nothing to be afraid of. I swear I am here to help you." I calmly seat myself on the rock, my arms folded across my chest. "Please, don't go yet," I say.

She scrambles to her feet and draws her forearm across her forehead, leaving a streak of mud.

"I admit I was surprised," I say. "I was a little shocked to find it was your own brother. But I am not shocked now." I take a deep breath. "You have a difficult road ahead of you. Before you go," I say, "I want to give you a healing blessing."

She stops again, seems to hesitate.

"You are not going to excommunicate me?" she asks.

"I don't know," I say, preparing her for my own purposes. "It all depends on how well you are willing to obey. You have to make a choice. Will you embrace God or the devil?" I gently ask.

She looks at my shoes, my belt, but will not lift her eyes to meet mine.

"You need two men for a proper blessing," she says.

"Yes," I say. "Sure. Technically, I do. But nobody else is here."

"It's okay?" she asks.

"God will fill the gap," I say. "He is the other person. There are two people in me—myself and God. We will bless you together."

It takes additional prodding to convince her of my good intentions, but in the end I am suave enough to manage it. I seat her on the rock. Going around behind her, I put one hand on each shoulder.

"State your full name," I say.

She tells me. I pour onto her head anointed oil from my pocket flask. I lay my hands upon her head and in God's name begin to bless her.

I bless her that she will not hate her brother, poor sinner that he is, and that she will worry only about her own sins. I bless her that she will know in God's eyes she is a daughter of goodness and that he loves her. I tell her that there is enough of God's grace even for the blackest of sinners and that, if she will hold to his path and not sway, God will save her, but she must trust God's chosen provost. In other words, me.

"Perhaps God's anointed will sometimes ask you to do things you do not understand or that you might at first think are wrong. You must trust him and do all he says without hesitation. Complete obedience is the only path to heaven. You must listen to your provost and follow his guidance in all things, and share nothing of what goes on privately between you and he. Not because it is secret or wrong, but because it is sacred."

I am going on in such fashion, laying her bare for my own purposes, when a refined and different logic begins to thump about my skull.

What do you want by associating yourself with a sinner of this pitch?

But I am a sinner myself, I respond. We are all of us sinners.

What might be sin to lesser people is no sin to you. Were what you do sin, God would have plucked you from your sacred office long ago. It must be no sin.

Surely inspired words straight from the Holy Spirit.

You may call me that.

I thought I had lost your guidance.

You'll never lose me.

The girl is becoming uncomfortable below me, shifting her head beneath the weight of my hands. I start to spout aloud again, letting the blessing flow where it will of its own accord, listening to the other thoughts swelling within me.

Don't soil yourself with this girl. She's committed the carnal act with her brother.

It wasn't her fault.

You need to save her.

How can I save her when I can't save myself?

The girl squirms again. I keep babbling and raise my voice higher. I fix my eyes on her bare neck.

Christ's blood will not wash her clean. She must atone for her sins with her own blood. Killing her is the best thing for her. Kill her to save her.

"I can't do it," I say. "I've never killed one before."

"Hunnh?" the girl says.

I am not asking you. I am commanding you.

"How do I know you are the Holy Spirit?"

"Are we finished?" the girl says.

Who else could I be?

"How do I know you are not the devil?"

"Who are you talking to?" the girl asks, her panic rising.

Examine me.

A vague figure flashes momentarily through my vision, a personage of white, an angel of light. Before I can get a closer look, it is gone.

"It's murder," I say, but there is no answer.

The girl struggles to rise. My hands slip off her head and down around her neck. I hold her until she is screaming and then I knock her head once hard against the rock. Her head turns odd and misshapen, losing form on one side. I pray privately for strength and am given it. I twist her neck until I am sure she is dead, and strip her of her clothes.

And then I rearrange her a bit so that her body will accommodate the spirit better. And then I go away.

CHAPTER 2

Breakfast

I embrace my wife. Kiss her on the cheek. She smiles limply before returning her attention to the stove.

I go to the table and sit down at the head of it, where the father is meant to sit. At the other end are my oldest and youngest children, the youngest in her high chair, the older girl feeding her.

"How's my pumpkin flower today?" I ask.

"Oh, Daddy!" says my eldest. She seems pleased and embarrassed, will not meet my gaze. She will grow into a real beauty, prettier even than the girl in the woods. I will be around to enjoy every minute of it.

My wife comes to table, sets before me a plate covered with a paper towel. Underneath it are strips of bacon, six, lined side by side, grease still bubbling upon them.

The twins come down the stairs together, stumbling over one another's feet.

"Good to see you, boys," I say heartily.

They look at each other and smirk.

"What is it?" I ask.

"Nothing," they say, both of them at once.

My wife brings the frying pan over to the table, begins dishing eggs overcooked and sticky with cheese onto the plates. She finishes, returns the pan to the stove, comes to sit down, tightening the sash of her bathrobe.

"Jack?" I say to one of the twins.

"What?" he asks.

"You know what," I say, making a show of pressing my palms together.

"Oh," he says. "Oh yeah."

He bows his head, stiffens his hands, the rest of us following.

"Our Father in Heaven," he prays. "Thank you for my family. Please bless the food. In the name of the Lamb, amen."

By the time I open my eyes, Jack has already grabbed his fork and started into his eggs, a long thread of cheese strung to his plate. He is a glutton. I will have to teach him to control his appetites or they will have the best of him.

"Has anyone seen the paper?" I ask.

"Jack, fetch your father the paper," says my wife.

"Why do I always have to do it?" Jack says. "I already had to say the prayer."

"Mark, get your father the paper," says my wife.

"Aww, Mom," says the other twin.

"Do as you're told, Mark," I say. "Don't talk back to your mother."

He gets up mumbling and stomps out of the room.

"Is anything wrong with the eggs?" my wife asks.

"No," I say. "Quite the contrary. These eggs are delicious."

"Don't feed me that," she says, frowning. "You haven't even tasted them."

I am considering how to respond in a way that will assert my authority when Mark returns with the paper, dropping it in my lap on the way past.

"There's your stupid paper," he says.

"Is that any way to talk to your father, Mark?" my wife asks.

Mark shrugs without looking at her. He climbs into his chair, begins to eat his eggs. I roll the rubber band off the newspaper, flatten the pages on the table. On the front page is a blurred spread of the girl's body, the privates, neck, and eyes marked out in solid black triangles. "Murder in the Woods" the headline reads.

"I think you should apologize," my wife says to Mark.

"No," I say. "That's okay. Maybe I shouldn't have made him get it."

My wife turns to me, looks at me hard. I gesture with my eyes down to the newspaper, turn the headline to face her way. She squints, examines it a moment, her pupils moving down the column.

"Oh my God," she says, and folds the paper closed.

"Mom!" says our eldest.

"Dad, Mom swore!" says Jack. "Don't swear, Mom."

"Not far from here," I say softly to my wife. "Just in the woods behind Barton's field. I'll have to go talk with the parents."

"Dad, who are you talking about?" says our eldest.

"Nothing," I say.

"I'm sorry I swore, Jack," my wife says. "It just came out."

"I think you should wash your mouth out with soap," says Mark.

"Mark," I say, "that's enough."

"Well, I do," he says.

"How old was she?" my wife whispers.

"Fourteen, I think," I say. I make a point of bringing my eggs onto my fork and pushing the fork into my mouth. "Yes, fourteen," I say.

"You guys just aren't making any sense," says Jack.

"We're not talking to you, Jack," I say.

"Who are you talking about?" my eldest yells.

"Nor to you," I say to her. "Stop asking questions and finish your breakfast."

"Do they know who did it?" my wife asks.

"No," I say. "But I think I might."

"You do? How do you know?"

"Did *what*?"

"Didn't I tell you to eat your breakfast?"

"I ate it already," my eldest says.

"Go upstairs and brush your hair," says my wife.

"It's combed," she says. "See?"

"It doesn't look combed," my wife says. "Comb it again. Go on."

"Mom!"

I put down my fork. "Listen to your mother," I say. "Upstairs."

My daughter makes a show of leaving, smashing her chair back into the wall, looking at us to see what we will say, climbing the stairs slowly, backwards, looking at us the whole time.

"You boys too," my wife says. "Go upstairs and get ready for school."

"I'm still eating, Mom," says Jack.

"Go," she says. "And wash your face."

Mark goes and Jack follows, groaning. My wife pulls Jack's plate onto the tray of our youngest's high chair. Our youngest takes up the plate, clatters it onto the floor. My wife gropes absently under the table for it, her eyes still on me, the baby grabbing at the clip in her hair.

"Who killed her?" my wife says.

"I shouldn't say anything," I say. "Clergy's confidentiality."

"Tell me anyway."

"I don't know for certain," I say. "If I tell you, I don't want to hear it from the neighbors when I get home tonight."

"Don't worry," she says. "I'll keep it to myself."

"I think it was her brother," I say.

"Her brother?"

"He got her pregnant. She told me herself."

"Her own brother?"

"Yes."

"Was it a half-brother?"

"How should I know? Would that make a difference? I think he was her full brother."

“Lord, that is awful,” she says. “But if he is capable of incest, he’s capable of murder.”

“We don’t know for certain he did it,” I say. “We shouldn’t judge the boy.”

“No,” she says. “I guess not.”

She opens the paper again, reading down the column, the picture of the girl in the clearing riding beside her thumb, staring at me. The girl is faceup in the photograph, though my recollection is facedown. I left her facedown, her body anyway. They’ve moved her head back around, away from where I left it, made it look still attached, ruining the tableau.

A pretty piece of work, if I do say so myself. But she’s saved. I’ve done her a favor.

“What are you going to do?” my wife asks.

“Go to the office. I should have left already.”

“About this, I mean,” she says, tapping the girl’s face. “About the brother.”

“I can’t prove any of it.”

“You should mention the brother to the police,” she says.

“Don’t tell me what to do,” I say. “I imagine they’ll figure it out on their own.”

“Go to them today,” she says.

“I shouldn’t have brought it up,” I say. “Forget I said anything.”

CHAPTER 3
Bus

I am proofreading a contract when a man chooses to sit next to me, although the bus is empty. He wears a white button-down shirt, a burgundy tie, a dark suit. He nods to me as he pulls his briefcase onto his lap, springing the catches, opening it up. He takes out the morning paper, unfolds the body of the dead girl.

"Morning," he says.

"Pardon?" I say.

"Morning," he says. "As in good morning."

"Yes," I say. "Good morning."

"Or as in bad morning," he says.

I shrug.

"Or as in mourning the dead," he says, tapping the girl's face.

"Yes," I say. "Terrible tragedy."

"No need to hold pretense with me," the man says. "Don't you recognize me?"

"I'm afraid I can't place you."

"Can it be you've forgotten me?" he asks. "Even after last night?"

"I was alone last night," I say. "I've never seen you before in my life."

"Don't remember me?"

"Can't you sit somewhere else?"

He looks perplexed. "Why this rough treatment?" he asks. "You were happy enough to take my advice last night, no?"

He sits back, stiff, examining the newspaper in his hands.

"'An act of extreme cruelty . . . ,'" he reads. "'Her neck broken.'" He turns to me. "Of course, they don't put all the details in there. They're saving some, things only the killer would know." He shakes the paper straight. "'It is unclear whether the rape occurred before or after her death. . . .'"

He raises his head. "Any comments?"

Lowering his head, he scans the rest of the article.

"Listen to this," he says. "'Police are confident that blood and semen samples will lead to the apprehension of the killer.'" He puts the paper down. "Think that over, Provost."

I turn toward the window and look out. The bus is passing out of the suburbs, past the park.

"I am not condemning you," the man says. "I am one of your greatest admirers. We've been through this," he says. "Let's move on to something new."

The bus turns, the back tire scraping the curb as it rounds the corner. I see an old man on his front porch, rocking, eyes missing. He waves slowly as the bus passes him. The man beside me waves absently back.

"You were right to tell your wife about the girl's brother," he says.

"But he didn't kill her."

"He's still guilty," he says. "Every day he was killing her. She wouldn't have had to be sanctified except for what he did to her. The way I see it you are blameless."

I get up and move back a few seats, the bus driver watching me in his rearview mirror. The man follows me back, pens me in.

"Tell the police about the brother, Provost," the man says. "Let them come to their own conclusions."

The buildings grow tall, become netted in wire and glass. The bus moves slower, but stays empty.

"I can't do it," I say.

"Can't?" he says. "Won't, you mean."

"He didn't kill her," I say.

"A technicality."

"Hardly."

"If he had been there maybe he'd have killed her. But for all the wrong reasons. It was fortunate you were there to kill her for the right ones."

Staring out the window, I think it over. I like the way it sounds.

On the sidewalk, a man looks at his watch, pushes his hair out of his face. On the sidewalk behind him a man in overalls seems to be shouting at someone though there is nobody paying him any heed.

"Look," the man beside me says. "Better him than you, no?"

The bus stops and two more people get on, two men in suits, wearing dark glasses. They pass the driver without him seeming to see them and start slowly back toward us.

"Got to go," the man next to me says. "Almost forgot. This is my stop."

He dashes from the seat and out the side door of the bus, the two men who have just climbed on rush down after him and out as well. I do not see him, but as the bus pulls out I see one of the other two speaking into a cellular phone, looking around as if confused. He catches a glimpse of me in the bus window and points. The bus pulls away.

In the late afternoon, the police call me at work, ask me if, as the girl's religious leader, I might have any information about the girl's murder.

"No," I say. "I don't believe I do."

"We were told that you might have some clue as to who the killer is."

"Who told you this?"

The officer on the other end of the line pauses. "I'd rather not reveal my source," he says. "Does it matter?"

"It might," I say. I am about to say more when the line clicks. "Just a moment, officer. Will you hold?" I say, and switch lines.

"Honey?" my wife says. "The police just called."

"I told you not to say anything."

"I'm sorry, it just came out."

"Why would they call at all?"

"Somebody thought they saw you near Barton's field that night," she says. "The police called about that. To see if you'd seen anything. One thing led to another."

"Me? I was never near there," I almost shout. "I swear."

"What's wrong?" she says. "I know that, you don't have to tell me, darling."

"I have to go," I say.

"I didn't mean to tell them," she says. "It just slipped out."

"Don't worry," I say. "I'll tell them what they should know."

CHAPTER 4

Interview

I have just finished my last evening interview and am closing the provost's office, sending my secretary Allen home, when I feel a hand on my shoulder. I turn to find my immediate ecclesiastical superior, the area rector, beside me. He regards me warmly.

"Rector Bates," I say. "How pleasant to see you."

"Greetings, Provost," he says. "Here late tonight?"

"Interviews," I say.

"You're finished?" he asks. "I wonder if you wouldn't mind coming down to my office a moment. I'd like a word with you."

"Of course," I say. "About what?"

"Personal," he says. "Come down when you have a moment."

I lock the door to the office, lock the building doors as well. I walk to the other end of the building, to the area offices, and knock on the door that has light seeping out from under it.

It takes a minute for the area rector to open the door. He ushers me inside, draws me around to a chair, then pulls a chair beside it for himself.

"Your wife mentioned you were here," he says. "Doing interviews. I figured now was as good a time as any." He presses his palms together between his knees. "I don't know how to bring this up," he says. "These things are never easy, and it's even more difficult considering your position in the Church. I think of you as a personal friend, Provost. I respect you. If I felt that I could get away without asking, I wouldn't ask," he says.

"I understand," I say. "You can ask me anything. I'll answer truthfully."

"The mothers of two boys in your congregation came to see me yesterday," he says. "They claim that you abused their sons."

I try to look surprised, shocked. "What? Me? What sort of abuse?"

"Sexual abuse of the worst kind."

"Sexual abuse? Me?"

"I couldn't believe it myself when she told me. Still can't. A Bloodite provost would never do such a thing. So I thought it would be best to ask you directly."

"I am glad you did," I say. "May I ask who has accused me?"

He considers a moment, then gives me the names of the mothers of two of the boys I have recently interviewed. Both boys, the spirit told me, had been abused by their uncles. In one case I was blameless. I did nothing but cleanse his body with my own so as to help him heal. In the other I was admittedly a little overeager, but the Lord has forgiven me.

"Those women have had a grudge against me since I was made provost," I say. "I'm not surprised."

"Is that so?" he says.

"I would have told you, but I never thought they would go this far."

"You deny the accusations, then?"

"Of course I deny them."

"You have never had any sort of history of abuse?"

By history, I assume he means have I ever been formally charged. "Never," I say.

"Look me in the eyes to tell me," he says.

I turn my head to look at him, find that he has opened his eyes wide, is staring me steadily down. It is theatrics, I know, the same tactics I use at times in my own interviews, but still I cannot help but feel the weight of his gaze. I dislike it. It makes me feel cornered, like an animal.

"I didn't do it," I say, holding my eyes steady.

"You wouldn't lie, would you?" he asks. "You know it is damnation to deceive the Lord over a matter of such magnitude, especially considering your ecclesiastical position."

"I am an honest man," I say.

"Look me in the eyes and tell me again," he says.

I look him straight in the eyes without flinching. "I have never abused anyone," I lie. "Sexually or otherwise."

He sits regarding me for several minutes.

"I believe you," he finally says. "That's all the proof I need. I would never have believed ill of you in any case. I was convinced of your innocence from the first."

"I am innocent," I say.

"You're the sort of man who could be an apostolic elder some day. That's what I've always thought. A shame how people accuse men of your caliber," he says. "Pure viciousness. You will have all the support I can muster."

"I bet those boys were never abused by anyone."

"No," he says. "One of the women has a medical report which documents it. It would make you sick to read it. At least one of the two boys was viciously raped. You didn't do it, but somebody did."

"Awful," I say. "Who would do such a thing?"

"Yes," he says. "Whoever did it deserves to be killed."

"Somebody in the neighborhood, perhaps?"

"Could be," he says. "I wouldn't be surprised. Maybe a relative." He crosses his legs. "I will tell the boys' mothers that I have thoroughly investigated the situation and find you blameless."

"If the women won't let it drop, will you let me know?" I ask.

"I will," he says. "I'll discourage them, try to convince them of their mistake. If they keep it up, I'll have to classify their behavior as unchristianlike conduct. We can excommunicate them for that. But I hope, for their sakes, they'll repent before it goes that far."

He stands up and thrusts his hand forward.

"Keep up the good work," he says.

"I will," I say, shaking his hand. "You can count on me."

CHAPTER 5

Funeral

I meet the dead girl's parents in my office at the church just before the funeral service. I shake hands all around, offering condolences to each member of the family.

"These are always the most difficult deaths to accept," I say. "Funerals for the young. It was not her time, but somebody chose to take her away from this life. You can be sure that the guilty will be punished by God."

The father nods, the rest of them too—even the brother, I see, expert at not revealing his guilt. He is a slippery character.

"The matter of the murder is in God's hands," I say. "You have to get past this. You cannot live on hate. You must live on love. There are questions likely never to be resolved for you about your daughter's death, questions for which neither you nor I will ever know the answer. You must let go."

The girl's mother, face tear run, nods. The children and the father remain sullen.

"Funerals should be a happy time," I say. "Even in circumstances such as these. Do not forget that your daughter is with God. That's something to be happy about."

We pray together and I stand holding the door open, shaking their hands as they file past. I stop the brother, grip his hand tightly.

"What's your name, son?" I ask.

"Josh," he says.

"Josh," I say. "Ah, yes. Your sister told me all about you."

A flicker of something passes near his mouth and quickly disappears.

"I doubt it," he says.

"Doubt not, fear not," I say. "Thus sayeth the Lord. Come visit me sometime."

"You don't know anything about me," he says.

He pulls his hand out of mine and steps out. I let the door swing shut.

As I gather my notes off the desk and take my Scriptures from the drawer, a knock comes from the window, from behind the curtains. I hold myself still, listen as the knock comes a second time, then a third.

I part the curtains. Outside, his face pressed against the glass, is a man.

I open the window, see the glass smeared with blood where his forehead was.

"Can I help you?" I ask.

He pulls his head straight and I see that there is an X hacked into his forehead. The hair of his head is shaved to the length of a day's growth of beard. His eyes are dark and penetrating, nervous.

"The question is, can I help you?" he says.

"I don't think so," I say, and begin closing the window.

He blocks me by placing his head in the gap. I can see all over the crown of his skull slits and streaks of blood, razor slashes.

"Can it be you don't recognize me?" he asks.

I go cold. I pull the window back and slam it against his head, opening a gash above his eye. Blood begins to drip onto the sill.

"I take it you aren't happy to see me again?"

"I've never seen you before in my life."

"How quickly we forget," he says. "The bus? Wednesday afternoon? And the woods before that?"

I look at him, his torn shirt, his faded jeans.

"No," I say. "You can't be."

"I can," he says. "I am."

"What happened to your clothes?"

"What?" he says. He looks down at his body, tugs up his T-shirt. "One takes whatever is available. I assumed you and I were close enough it wouldn't matter." He looks back to me. "Or shall we say I am traveling incognito?" he asks. "That I am trying to avoid someone?"

"Avoid who?"

"Aren't you going to invite me in?" he asks.

"I have a funeral service to conduct."

"I am here to help," he says. "There are things that should be said at this funeral. I am just the man to say them."

"You?"

"Why not?" he says. "Invite me inside."

"You aren't dressed for a funeral."

"This?" he says. "Don't worry about this. Nobody will mind."

I stand staring out at him.

"Invite me in," he says. "The people would much rather listen to me than to you."

I stand hesitating, fingering my notes.

"Do you really trust yourself not to slip?" he asks. "What are you going to feel when you see her casket?"

"Come in," I say. "But only for a minute."

He pushes the window fully open with his hand, then reaches out to me. I extend my hand, pull him up onto the sill and through.

"You can't stay long," I say.

"Once I'm in, I'm in," he says. "Nobody tells me how long I can stay."

He opens the door and goes out, ushering me before him. I step out and into the foyer, find it empty, the doors to the chapel proper shut. Opening these doors, he waves me in.

The whole congregation is seated. They turn their heads as I enter, following me with their eyes as I walk up the aisle and onto the platform. The family is already seated on the stand. In the front and to the side, near the sacrament table, is the casket, lid screwed down, gleaming.

I can see my face in its skin. I cannot take my eyes away from the face, distorted and rippling.

I feel a hand tight upon my arm, the bloody-headed man tugging me toward the stand.

"You see?" he says. "You could never make it through the service without me."

"I don't know."

"Sit up there and keep your mouth shut," he says.

I let him drag me up the steps and to my seat. I sit, heavy and awkward.

"Where is the program?" he asks.

I hand him the mimeographed half-sheet of paper, a picture of Jesus and the open tomb on one side, the program notes on the other. He squints at it and approaches the microphone, taps on it.

"Is this thing on?" he asks.

After this, I don't know what happens. I know that he is speaking, can hear him utter phrases, can hear the individual words and tones, but the words do not seem to string together properly. He is babbling and I am in dread of how I will be able to repair the damage.

But, as I wait, I realize that the audience seems to be swallowing his words well enough. They regard him intently and do not turn away. They do not seem displeased, and many are moved to tears by his words. They seem to hang on his every phrase.

I turn to one side, touch the girl's father sitting next to me.

"What is he saying?" I ask. "Can you make any sense of it?"

The father does not seem to notice my touch. He stays still, his eyes welling with tears, watching the man with the blood-streaked head.

I look around. People throughout the chapel are similarly transfixed.

I watch it go on, the bloody-headed man speaking himself hoarse, the crowd fixing him in their attention with the utmost relentlessness. I look to the wall clock, watching the second hand spin slowly. I look out the side window, through marbled glass. A small dark shape is there, on the outside, where I know a bird is making a nest. I make a mental note to have the janitor remove it.

I nudge the girl's father.

"How long is he going to speak?" I ask.

The father does not seem to notice me.

"Does he know he isn't making any sense?" I shout in the father's ear.

When there is no response, I turn again to Bloody-Head, listen carefully to his words. There are the words "awful blood," among others. Or it might be "lawful blood." And "redemption" and "love," but nothing that comes together of a piece in and of itself.

I shake my head to clear it. It does not come clear.

I look past him and see the gleaming lid of the coffin, a long narrow blur on it that I believe to be the remains of my face. As I examine it, it seems to me my face and my body too, and myself and the girl in the woods.

The doors at the back of the chapel swing to either side and two men enter wearing dark suits and tinted glasses. The bloody-headed man at the pulpit stops abruptly, looks back to me, turns back to watch them come.

They approach slowly, unnoticed by the crowd, one of them speaking into a cellular telephone. Bloody-Head starts speaking faster, pounding his fist on the pulpit. The two come onto the stage, approaching him from either side.

"I suppose this is your doing?" says one of the men, pointing his finger at me.

"Me?" I say.

"Don't think you are getting away with anything," he says.

The other man has holstered his telephone so as to strike the bloody-headed man in the face. The bloody-headed man grips the podium tightly, keeps speaking as the other man hits him again, his colleague does so as well. With their fists they hammer his fingers until he can no longer hold to the podium. The audience seems not to notice. They knock him down. He keeps speaking.

They take the bloody-headed man under the arms, drag him from the stand as he struggles, continuing with the speech well down the aisle.

"Is this how you allow your guests to be treated?" he calls toward me.

I stand to see him better. He breaks away an instant, darts for the podium but is overwhelmed by the other two men before he arrives. They strike him a few times in the face and begin to drag him away down the aisle, backwards, his heels flopping along the floor.

"I'll see you later, Provost," he calls back to me.

"Don't count on it," says one of the men in dark glasses.

"You will have to finish yourself," calls the bloody-headed man. "Don't say anything stupid. Speak in tongues of flame or not at all!"

They push the chapel doors open and leave.

All of a sudden, I find myself before the podium, staring at the coffin, the image of my face. The crowd below seems restless.

"Where was I?" I ask. "What was I saying?"

The crowd pulls back visibly in their seats. A few of them begin to converse neighbor to neighbor, whispering among themselves, looking at me oddly.

"Someone please tell me," I say.

They fall silent. I realize that I am holding a program of the meeting in my hand. I read aloud the first thing my eyes see.

I sit down. The girl's father leans over, whispers into my ear, "You can't end the service yet."

I have to get him to show me where on the program we are. I stand and announce shakily that the girl's brother will speak. I sit back in my seat, marking and holding with my thumb the next item on the program, the meeting dragging along, words labored and falling all around us until at last it is over.

I stay beside the grave as the other mourners leave, stay with the family as they consider the coffin, the heap of earth beside it. I sprinkle earth on the coffin, to ruin the reflection. The family, thinking it to be a ritual, follows suit.

There are, I can see, two men behind the trees, observing us. Plainclothesmen.

I signal to the men by touching an elbow. They each touch their brow. By their signs ye shall know them.

I give my final condolences to the family in gestures, without touching them, as the other mourners scatter around us. To the brother, however, I reach out and take both his hands in my own, squeeze them.

"This must be difficult for you," I say. "More than the others, perhaps."

Before he can respond I have left them, am walking away.

"What do you want from me?" the brother yells after me.

I walk a few more steps and then turn back to look, see the two officers step out from among the trees and move toward the family. From the bushes I observe the family again take dirt in their hands and sprinkle the coffin. Far behind them the caretaker fires up an earthmover. The family begins to walk, the two men following from behind.

They are only a few steps distant when the two men stop them, show their badges. The family looks confused, seems to be looking around for someone to save them. The men take a position to either side of the brother, speak to him at length, the rest of the family crowding around.

The boy starts shaking his head, the mother shrieks. The boy suddenly darts away and starts to run. He comes crashing through the bushes near me without seeing me, runs past. The two men come after him. I point them in the proper direction, listen to the sounds of their pursuit.

CHAPTER 6

Nights

I wake to find a dark shape spread above me, shaking me. I lash out, carry my fist through it hard. It falls to one side, dully strikes the floor.

I grope under the bed but find nothing to strike it with a second time. Stumbling from the bed, I turn on the lamp, my fist aching.

My wife is on the far side of the bed, on the floor, unconscious, a discolored mark rising from her forehead.

"Jesus," I say. "I thought you were the devil."

I lift her onto the bed and stroke her face until she starts to regain consciousness. She looks at me without knowing me, tries to scramble free.

I hold her still.

"I'm here," I say. "I'm here."

She stops struggling, looks at me oddly.

"What happened?" she asks.

"You're safe," I say. "Close your eyes."

When she does, I get out of the bed and take a washcloth from the bathroom. I soak it with water and wring it out, then fill it with ice in the kitchen. I take it back to the bedroom, apply it to her forehead. She winces, then starts to cry.

"You hit me," she says.

"What makes you think I hit you?" I ask.

"I watched you," she says. "Why did you hit me?"

"I was hardly awake. I didn't know what I was doing."

"I didn't know you could hit so hard."

I shrug. "I wasn't awake."

She closes her eyes.

"Leaning over me like that," I say. "I thought you were the devil."

She doesn't respond, just lies there with the washcloth pressed to her forehead, shaking.

"Are you crying?" I ask.

"It hurts," she says. "It really hurts."

I lie down next to her, throw an arm across her, my upper leg passing over her hips.

"I need to sleep," I say. "I have a full day tomorrow."

She is, I can feel from the way her belly vibrates, from the wet smell of her breath, still crying. I don't say anything. I pretend I am falling asleep. And then I do fall asleep.

"Are you awake, honey?" she asks.

I don't say anything, don't move.

"Are you awake?" she asks again.

"Starting to be," I say.

"Sorry," she says. "I didn't mean to wake you."

"I am awake now."

"I need to talk to you. I need you to tell me everything will be okay."

"Everything will be okay."

"Don't just say it: talk about it."

"What do you want me to say?"

"You were saying the most awful things in your sleep," she says. "Things I couldn't bear to hear. And in the strangest voice."

"What was I saying?"

"I don't want to talk about it," she says.

"Then why did you wake me?"

"I don't want to say them."

"Tell me," I say. "They didn't mean anything, but I want to know."

"It was about that poor girl who was killed in the woods," she says. "You were talking dirty to her."

"That's nonsense," I say. "You're crazy."

"You were telling her what you were going to do with her. You talked dirty and then you told her you would kill her."

"It was a dream," I say. "It doesn't mean a thing."

"It frightened me," she says. "I couldn't believe you would say what you said, even in your sleep."

"Look," I lie. "Maybe I can't help thinking that if I had reported the brother to someone none of this would have happened. Maybe I feel responsible for her death because of that."

We lie still for some time, touching without moving.

"Maybe that's it," she says. "I might be able to live with that."

"It was an awful thing her brother did," I say. "And then to kill her over it."

I roll over in the bed, toward the wall.

"There is something else I want to ask you," she says.

"What?"

"When you came home the night the girl was murdered the knees of your pants were muddy. Your shoes too. There was some blood as well. Not much, but it was there."

I am fully awake now.

"That's not a question," I say.

"Why, darling?" she asks. "Can't you tell me why?"

"Why?" I say. "I stopped on the way to the church to play football with some kids, that's why."

"You were late, you said. You said you couldn't stay and take the baby out of the bath."

"Just a play or two," I say. "On the way. It didn't slow me down any. They threw me a pass downfield and I slipped."

She doesn't say anything.

"Don't you believe me?" I ask. "Do you think I would still be the provost if I could lie? Do you think God would tolerate it?"

"I don't know," she says.

"You have to put your faith in God," I say. "And in his earthly representatives. Doubt not, fear not."

"Who did you see that night?" she asks. "For the appointment, I mean."

"I was at the church."

"Who did you meet at the church?"

"I can't say," I say. "The interview was confidential. Someday, when things are less sensitive, I'll tell you all about it. But you've already proven you can't keep a secret."

"Don't say that," she says.

"You'll have to trust me." I take her in my arms, feel the bones in her back. "You have everything to lose and nothing to gain."

"Promise me you had nothing to do with that girl's death."

"I had nothing at all to do with that girl's death," I say. "May God strike me down if I am lying."

She is silent long enough that I think she must have fallen asleep. I am falling asleep myself when she says:

"I think you ought to see someone."

"What do you mean?"

"A psychiatrist. You are feeling things you shouldn't be feeling."

"I don't know," I say.

"It's coming out in your sleep," she says. "It isn't healthy. You need somebody to work through this with you."

I consider. If I keep talking in my sleep, I will give enough of the truth away that she will have a hard time dismissing it.

"Do it for me, honey," my wife says.

"Okay," I say. "Anything for you."

CHAPTER 7

Therapy

"Fochs," the therapist says. "Interesting name. German? Long *O* or short? Mine is German too: Feshtig. And a provost for the Church of the Blood of the Lamb no less."

"Yes," I say. "Appointed almost a year ago now."

"Good for you," he says. Reaching his hand out, he draws me into his office. "Please, sit where you'd like."

I look around. There are several chairs, a bench, a teak desk, a chair on casters.

"I don't care where I sit," I say.

"Chair, then?" he asks, and gestures. I choose a chair and sit, and he sits across from me. It feels as if the floor is yawning open between us.

We sit looking at one another, until I smile and look away. I look at his shelves, the books there, all titles I do not recognize. I look at his desk, its surface spare, almost devoid of objects.

He asks me if he can tape our meeting and I tell him yes. He turns on the tape recorder and we chat for a while, general information. When it starts getting personal, I steer him away. He sits looking at me, waiting.

"I filled out a form up front," I say. "It says why I'm here. Did they give it to you?"

"Tell me," he says.

"Well," I say. I consider what to say, how to phrase it. How much of the truth I can tell him without things getting messy. "I have been having bad dreams."

"What sort of bad dreams?"

"More like disturbing thoughts and feelings," I say. "The dreams came later. I imagine myself doing awful things and sometimes I can convince myself I have actually done them. Though, really, I never do them," I say.

"Tell me about these thoughts and feelings," he says.

"I think," I say. "I think it all started when I was called to be provost. They called me to be provost but I'm not really worthy. I'm not the kind of person that should be provost."

"Why not?"

"If I was the right kind of person, I wouldn't be having thoughts and feelings like these, would I?"

"What sorts of thoughts and feelings are they?"

"About children," I say. "My guess is they are a result of feelings of inadequacy over being called to be provost. I'm certain of it."

"So the thoughts tell you that you aren't worthy to be provost because provosts don't have such thoughts, but at the same time they didn't start until after you became a provost?"

"Yes," I say, though it sounds odd when he phrases it that way.

"They didn't start before you were provost?"

"Before?" I say. "Never."

He makes a note to himself on a pad of paper.

"What do you mean improper?" he asks.

"You know. Wrong thoughts."

"What makes them wrong?"

Some people need everything spelled out for them it seems. I consider how most people would respond to this, then feign discomfort, as if I am reluctant to speak.

I realize I have not thought enough about how I should proceed. I mumble out noncommittal responses until the questions turn elsewhere. He asks me questions about my parents, but I know I don't want to tell him the truth. I begin to make up a family for myself, the family I would have liked to have had growing up. This goes on for a while until I worry I am making up more than I can keep track of. I stop answering or answer vaguely though he keeps prodding, until finally he stops, looks at me closely.

"I'd like to try something unorthodox," he says, or something like that. "Do you mind following me along?"

I must admit, I am curious. "Why not?" I say.

"If I say to you, you're no longer a person, you're an object, what's the first object that comes to mind?"

"Well," I say. "I don't know. A slice of paper I suppose."

It's the second thing that comes to mind and I don't think it means anything, except maybe for "slice," which comes out because knife is the first thing that comes to mind. He begins to question me and I answer as I can, slowly realizing that with a little explanation the image is as good as any other. I have two sides, but only one can be seen at a time. I've never felt like I had an inside, always felt like I was on top of my skin rather than down inside of it. I have never felt any sense of something inside nor, quite frankly, a sense of something beyond. What matters is what I can touch and feel, the surface of my skin shaping itself to meet the objects around it. The soul is tactile and comes and goes.

To think such thoughts makes me feel like I am hovering over the edge of a great void. I realize I am learning about myself something that, finally, I am not certain I care to know.

"All I want," I offer, "is for you to cure me of my thoughts."

"I understand," he says. "But sometimes these things take time. What we need is to determine what lies behind the thoughts, what made you have them. That's the only way to make them leave you for good."

"The thoughts come from my feelings of unworthiness about being a provost," I say. "I told you that already."

"Yes," he says. "Perhaps. What we must discover, then, is what exactly makes you uneasy about being a provost. Why is your uneasiness manifested in this fashion instead of another?"

I know I have no interest in allowing him to uncover the truth. I have come to see him not because I am interested in him discovering what I am, but because I need, in some form, to vocalize what I have been doing to children over the last decade, and what in particular I have done in the last few months. I have kept too much inside and it is beginning to spill out. I need to release some of it.

So, I will meet with him a few times. So, I will talk the worst of it out, under the premise, for him, that I am speaking not of anything I have actually done but merely of my thoughts and dreams and fears. I will lighten the load a little, I will brag a little, I will enjoy myself. And then, when he comes a little too close to the truth, I will cut off treatment, go home to my wife, and sleep soundly, without dreams.

PART THREE
FURTHER RESEARCH

Aaron P. Blanchard, Apostolic Elder
The Corporation of the Blood of the Lamb
Church Headquarters Facility, Floor 25

Doctor Feshtig,
It has come to my attention that you are preparing a summary of Provost Fochs's case. I must counsel you that it is not felt to be in the best interest of the Church for you to publish such a study. If you choose to publish, there will be severe repercussions.

Because of the sensitive nature of the Fochs case, I must insist you allow the Church to have full access to your notes. I must require as well that you share them with no one else until the Committee for the Strengthening of the Church has examined them fully and made any necessary modifications.

I know you will not be pleased about this, but I must insist you obey. Please understand the public furor it would cause both within the Church and outside of it if the internal disturbances and delusions of a provost were made known. The reputation of the Church must be upheld.

If you go to the Lord in prayer, you will reach the same conclusion I have and will forward your notes as per my request. If you are unable to cooperate, I must ask for your resignation from the Zion Foundation.

Yours in Christ,
Elder Aaron P. Blanchard

Alexander Feshtig
Zion Foundation Institute of Psychoanalysis

Elder Blanchard:
I do not know how you managed to gain access to my preliminary study of Fochs. Quite frankly, I don't care to know. There is always someone willing to serve the Lord who feels that his obedience to God justifies taking every liberty.

I have seen this coming for some time. The claims you yourself publicly make for the freedom of the Zion Foundation, for our ability to operate separately from the Church, are obviously empty. I am disappointed with you, with the Church, and with our foundation.

Despite all claims the Corporation of the Blood of the Lamb makes to be a divinely inspired Church, it seems oddly as eager as any worldly institution to soil its hands in a little impropriety, to cover a few things over if that means furthering the cause of righteousness. What happens to the claims of divine guidance at such moments? Can such guidance be flicked on and off like a lightbulb? Do you believe you can hide from God?

What few of my files you have will do you little good: the provisional evaluation in them was based on the belief that what Fochs described as his disturbing dreams, thoughts, and feelings were indeed restricted to dream, thought, and feeling. But I have discovered enough since writing that initial study to realize that Fochs's "dreams" and "thoughts" are in fact real experiences, acts he has committed. It is much worse than you thought, Elder: you do not have a disturbed provost who is thinking shocking thoughts; you have a provost involved in the destruction of children, who feels no remorse, and who has used his church position to prey on children. Was "divine guidance" accidentally switched off when Fochs was called to be provost?

I want my papers returned without delay. As to your suggestion that I resign, I have no intention of doing so. But I will not cooperate either.

Sincerely,
Feshtig

Aaron P. Blanchard, Apostolic Elder
The Corporation of the Blood of the Lamb
Church Headquarters Facility, Floor 25

Director Kennedy,
It is of the utmost importance that I obtain all materials related to Doctor Feshtig's analysis of Provost Fochs. A great deal is at stake, none of which I am at liberty to discuss. I would suggest you do all you can to accommodate the Lord in this matter.

I understand you had a certain amount of difficulty obtaining the materials you have already sent. Trust me when I say further papers must be obtained by whatever means possible, even means that, in normal circumstances and without the direction of the Lord, both you and myself would shy away from. It is at crossroads such as these that those who truly love the Lord, those who are willing to serve his Church with all their might, mind, and strength, distinguish themselves from the common herd.

I command you to take any and all action you deem appropriate toward the resolution of this matter. Though I in no way care to have my name or the Church's name associated with whatever course of action you choose to undertake, and though I would prefer not to be appraised of the details, trust that the Church will always be there to uphold and defend you.

Yours in Christ,
Elder Blanchard

Alexander Feshtig
Zion Foundation Institute of Psychoanalysis

Elder Blanchard,

I was summoned this morning for an urgent interview with my provost. When I arrived, I was made to understand that my worthiness to be a member of the Bloodite faith was being called into question. I was told that someone had reported that in my psychiatric practice I was "preaching a vision of the world and the soul contradictory to the true vision offered by the restored gospel of Jesus Christ." He said that he had been told that I had "resisted helping the Church" in my professional capacity and that I was "openly preaching a nihilistic rejection of the soul that contradicted the Church's recent Statement in Support of Family Values." When I questioned him as to who had raised these charges, he at first would not say, but did indicate that it was "somebody worth listening to." After a great deal of prodding, he reluctantly admitted it had been you.

It seems you are trying to intimidate me into cooperating. Clearly you have no compunction against avoiding all proper channels and inflicting your will on a provost in awe of your authority: someone who is, for you, a disposable token in a game of power.

As to your accusations regarding my world view, it is true that I do not attempt the same sort of simpleminded synthesis of the gospel and the psychiatric profession as would someone like Director Kennedy with his so-called "Christianalysis." Kennedy is, quite frankly, in flight from an understanding of the self, using clichés and the worst religious inspirational propaganda to paper over people's problems. He does considerable damage to his patients, distancing them from the possibility of cure.

I will not have someone who knows absolutely nothing about my profession dictate what my actions should be in regard to my patients. I will not allow my integrity to be ground up in the gears of the Church just to keep from getting on your bad side.

It is clear that you are covertly encouraging my local provost to have me excommunicated. I ask you to have the dignity to confront me directly instead of hiding behind my provost, pretending that these decisions are being made locally rather than at a higher level.

You shall have no further information on Fochs unless you go through proper channels and receive permission from Fochs himself. Until then, there is no justification for sharing anything with you. I will not do so.

Feshtig

Memorandum, Zion Foundation Institute of Psychoanalysis
From: Feshtig
To: Kennedy

I arrived at my office this morning to be confronted by your clumsy attempt to simulate a burglary to gain access to my papers. You have, of course, what you wanted (or rather what the Church—i.e., Blanchard—wanted), but consider, Kennedy, what you have had to sacrifice to gain it.

The next time you attempt this, you would do well to keep the following in mind:

—You took only my Fochs file. When you are simulating a burglary, you should take more than just the item you are after. You're a psychologist, for Christ's sake. Can't you at least make some pretense of actually thinking like a burglar?

—Usually a burglar has to have a way in. In this case, the door was locked, the windows unbroken. Am I to believe that the burglar picked the lock, overturned my furniture, pried my private cabinet open with a crowbar, took Fochs's papers, and then carefully locked the door as he left?

Kennedy, you are obviously not cut out for burglary. This is serious business. Stop and consider where this is leading you. In a short period of time, you have begun, in the name of God, to sacrifice all your ethics. Where will you draw the line? It is apparently acceptable for you to lie and steal. Why stop there? What is there to restrain you from killing someone if Blanchard asks it? Are you comfortable believing that the Church will never ask that of you, just as you were comfortable not long ago believing that Blanchard would never ask you to do anything dishonest.

Are you willing to turn your life over to a leader who is eager to abuse your willingness to be used?

In any case, congratulations. You have found in my office enough to keep Blanchard happy for a few hours. You should be proud of yourself. He'll leave you alone. At least until he needs something else.

Feshtig

Notebook

Some thoughts and further discomfort about my (ex)patient Fochs. His dreams have an alarming habit of resurfacing as news stories. In the newspaper today, two mothers claim their boys were sexually abused by one Provost Fochs, six months ago. The particulars correspond with Fochs's dream of the two boys in all important points.

My responses complicated by Kennedy's unexplained interest in the Fochs case. I am looking harder for ghosts than perhaps I should.

Listening again to the Fochs tapes, speeding through. Strikes me differently when I hear his disembodied voice—something disingenuous about his words that his presence masked from me before. Though perhaps I am reading into his voice what I expect (and fear) to find.

Calls to Fochs's office, two attempted through the secretary, one by myself from the gas station on the way home. Never an answer.

A bad night. J. gone to spend weekend with his mother and me left alone in the house, no moon, the windows black and expressionless. Even when I press my face to them I can hardly see out. I keep going out to stare at the yard until my eyes slowly adjust to the dim shapes, then back inside again.

A dream of my own, stolen from Fochs's repertoire. The girl's head hanging back between the shoulders, a pulpy sack. No more than that, a frozen sepia locket, slowly fading from vision and falling asunder.

I awoke terrified and stumbled about the house, turning on all the lights.

Not worth interpreting.

Called Fochs, no answer. Hiked in the morning, up through the aspens to where I could see the whole smog-ridden valley spread below. A smudged but dizzying prospect.

...

I drove across town to the address Fochs had listed on the clinic's forms. No home there, only an empty and overgrown lot humming with grasshoppers.

I tried the telephone number again, received no answer. Opening the telephone book, I looked up *Fochs, Eldon.* He was not listed in any of the communities in the book. I should have thought to demand the name of his congregation, though most likely he would have lied about that as well.

There was, though, in nearby Carswell, a Myra and Zina Fochs. Farm Route 12, #4. I wrote the address down.

Trouble at work, Kennedy angry with me. I am the one who should be angry with him.

J. retrieved. Briefly uncomfortable for me to see my former wife, but over quickly. J. spoke nonstop and with great nervousness all the way home.

I dialed Myra and Zina Fochs's number. An answering machine picked up and a male voice I didn't recognize asked me to leave a message. I considered, then hung up.

Probably it will lead nowhere, but it is all I have. It is only a half hour drive to Carswell. I will go tomorrow.

In the evening, after leaving work, I drove down Farm Route 12. At the fourth mailbox, there was a small house on a large property, fields behind and to either side. The man who opened the door was in his forties. Blond hair spilled over into his eyebrows. He wore a battered felt shirt and stitched cowboy boots, his skin pleated and red from sun.

"I'm looking for Mr. Fochs," I said.

"Looking at him. I'm Myra Fochs."

I introduced myself and apologized, explained I was looking not for him but for another fellow by the name of Fochs.

"Oh?" he said. "Not many Fochses around anymore, and nearly all that are are related. Who you looking for?"

"Eldon Fochs."

He looked at me a little strangely, demanded again to know who I was. I was a psychiatrist who had been working with Mr. Fochs, I explained, and who needed to get in contact with him.

"I suppose you better come on in," he said.

Inside, the house was simple and small, the furniture covered with flowered sheets that had been pleated to hug them. The walls were a pine, stained orangish-brown. A small, ceramic plaque of a bear was on the wall, along with a lacquered bullwhip, a spread lariat, and a picture of a smiling old man in a black Stetson.

A woman, around the same age as Myra, sat awkwardly below the picture. She stood to greet me, touching her hair, smoothing her skirt.

"It's about Eldon," the man said to her.

"Oh Lord," she said, and left the room.

He sat down in an easy chair, motioned me to the sheet-covered couch.

"I try to keep my distance now," he said. "We never were close. We got different ways of being in the world."

Leaning forward in his chair, he craned his neck to one side. He unbuttoned his shirt and tugged it back away from his neck. Underneath, along his clavicle and down into his chest, were three dark parallel scars.

"That's his work," he said. "Eldon's, I mean. Did it with this kind of tool he made for himself out of wood and barbed wire. Long, skinny job, stiff and sharp. Saw him do in a rockgut with it too."

"Rockgut?"

"Sure," he said. "Prairie dogs they get called as well." He buttoned his collar up. He sat still for a moment, just looking at me, then rolled up his pant leg, showed a portion of his calf where the skin was a scarlet band, dauped and irregular.

"That's his work too," he said. "He got me tied up one time when we were kids and had Frank's cattlecutter and some tongs he stole, and started cutting and tearing. Was going to fry it up, but Frank caught him first."

"Who's Frank?"

"That's the stepdad. He was okay mostly. That's him in the picture," he said, pointing to the Stetsoned man.

"What's your connection to Eldon?"

"Why, he's my brother."

"He told me he was an only child."

Myra snorted. "He never did like any of us much."

"How many are there?"

"Let's see. Three at first: Eldon first and me second and Janeen third—she's a girl, a woman now—and then Momma went and divorced Daddy. Then Frank showed and dragged in two more about my age, and he and my mother decided to have one more just for good measure. All three of those have a different name, though. Bidwell. Only me and Janeen and Eldon were Fochses. Why'd Eldon come to see you anyway?"

"He was disturbed about some dreams he'd been having."

He shook his head. "Eldon never was disturbed by nothing I know," he said. "He could do just about any goddamn thing without a flinch to him."

Myra got up suddenly, went to stare out the window, then came and sat down again and looked at his hands.

"Eldon and I don't talk," he said. "I could tell you why, but I don't hardly know you."

"Did you know your brother was a provost?"

"I'm not surprised. Just one more thing to make me glad I'm free of the Church. Eldon, he always was one to put on the pretty good face in public. Momma never would believe anything bad of him, even when I had that skin hanging off my leg. I don't have no use for the Church anyway. I was always of Frank's mind over that."

"Do you take a newspaper?"

"You trying to sell me the paper?"

"Your brother was in the newspaper recently. I wondered if you'd seen it. He was accused of raping two boys."

Myra got up and went to the window again. Came back and sat down.

"Like I say," he said. "Eldon and I don't talk."

"You think he did it?"

"I told you we don't talk no more."

"I'm just asking your opinion."

"I was even his own brother and I knew a lot about him but there was a lot he kept hidden from me. Maybe even from himself. I don't know the why of it. He was just always uneasy inside, and he never could get easy with himself."

"You think he could have done it?"

"I'm not about to talk on that subject no more."

"What was your father like?"

"Daddy or Frank?"

"Your real father."

"Daddy? He was a churchgoer, straight as a level. Could batter you pretty hard if you got out of plumb or even if you didn't. Eldon got most of it, though. Hear Frank tell it, one time Daddy even picked up the spade and smacked him on the head so hard that some of his brains leaked out his nose. But Momma divorced from him before he could do me much harm."

"Your father was a provost?"

He nodded. "His whole life was the Church. Momma took hell from everybody for divorcing him. Eldon looked up to him in spite of everything. Me, I was mostly raised by Frank. He was never a believer. Eldon, he was the oldest, got a full dose of religion and maybe even believes it still."

"Did your father sexually abuse him?"

"Excuse me?"

"I don't mean to pry," I said.

"I don't have an answer to a question like that," he said. "I just don't."

"Please," I said. "I've only a few more questions. If they're too personal, you don't have to answer them."

He looked at me long, without expression. Then he looked around the room, at the picture, at the lariat, at the base of the couch. "All right," he said. "What the hell."

"Did Eldon ever kill anybody?"

"No chance," he said. He kept shaking his head. "Killed animals when he was a kid, though," he finally said. "Killed our cat by twisting its head mostly off. Had a thing with heads and animals—sometimes didn't like to see the two together. Used to find stray dogs too and lop their paws off. Most people were just glad that someone was getting rid of the strays, so they didn't ask no questions."

"What if I were to tell you Eldon might have killed someone?"

"I'd ask you what you're doing here talking to me instead of talking to the police."

"If your brother is to be held responsible, you'll have to help. I need you to speak with the police."

He sat regarding his hands.

"It's not your brother," he said.

"You wouldn't have to say much," I said. "Just the truth."

"I don't know you at all," he said. "You're probably crazy for all I know. Besides, they're all good Bloodites around here. They protect their own, especially if he's a provost."

"Please," I said.

He got up from his chair, opened the door.

"Can't help you," he said. "Nothing personal, just can't."

Was awakened at dawn today, the sun burning through the slats, the talk with Fochs's brother still awash in my head. Went in and looked at J. for a while, sleeping blankly. It could have as easily been J. as those two other boys, given the right circumstances and the wrong provost.

I thought that over awhile, then went downstairs and cooked and dressed and woke J. and left.

...

Between patients scanned again the newspaper article on Fochs's alleged abuse of two boys. The names of the two boys were withheld, though the full names of the two mothers were printed, making the withholding of the boys' names pointless. The last name of one of the mothers is Young, too common, but the last name of the other is Mears, hardly a common name at all.

I looked the name up in the directory, called the only listing, spoke to the boy's mother. We've agreed to meet.

A letter from an apostolic elder, Blanchard, out of nowhere and without warning, raising the stakes. I am, he informs me, not to publish anything about the Fochs case nor to discuss it with anyone. If I do, I will lose my job.

It seems someone, Kennedy surely, has given him some of my Fochs papers, my preliminary work. What he doesn't realize is how faulty the conclusions of that study are. Fochs, I am now convinced, did much, perhaps all, of the things he described as thoughts and dreams. He is not merely a mentally confused provost: he is a pedophile and perhaps even a killer.

Wrote an aggressive reply back. Perhaps a mistake to do so—it might cost me my church membership. But once you start giving in, you never stop.

Met with Patricia Mears, the mother of one of the boys (Nathan) that Fochs allegedly abused. Very cooperative, her husband as well. They were certain that Nathan had told the truth. She gave me a thick packet of documents, ranging from the original medical report and a transcript of conversations between Nathan and Patty about the abuse, to an account of Patty's excommunication because she refused to let the matter drop. This latter account included a summary of the church court proceedings, which contained a number of inconsistencies and procedural irregularities. Also in the packet, a three-by-five card to which was taped a hair found inside Nathan's sweater after the rape, next to it a hair sample from Fochs.

The lab report revealed the coloring and composition were identical. Fochs, however, had argued that since he had interviewed Mears on the day of the rape, the hair could have easily passed onto him during that time, that it was no indication that he had raped the boy.

I asked them why they had withdrawn charges. It was too hard on Nathan, they said. It was humiliating. He couldn't bear the strain.

I asked them if they felt there was a single incident or if the abuse had been a repeated practice. Patricia said she did not know. She said that Fochs had met frequently with the youth. He had often come to visit Nathan and had invited him and other children over to his house for evening discussions, particularly on evenings when his wife was absent. She had thought nothing of it: since Fochs was a provost it seemed natural for him to pay close attention to the youth. He seemed above suspicion. All she could say for certain was that the time they had discovered the abuse was the only time in which the physical damage done to Nathan had been severe enough that he could not hide it, though he had tried. The father said that it had made them reconsider every time Nathan had been with Fochs. They believed that yes, this was not the first time.

I asked them if they had noticed sudden shifts in Nathan's behavior. They indicated that his personality had changed dramatically in the course of the last year, that he had been increasingly anxious and withdrawn. They thought at first this was part of puberty and becoming a teenager. Now, though, they were unsure what to think.

Woke in a sweat and with a premonition about J. Rushed down to find him sleeping peacefully. Returned to bed, heart still pounding.

Met briefly with Nathan, somewhat informally. He was reluctant to speak, frightened, nervous. Slowly he is learning to trust me.

It is clear now that with Fochs I let his being a provost disarm me slightly. There are things I should have noticed about him that I didn't. Now, at least, I have a chance to make amends.

Yanked out of Sunday school today by my provost, who tells me he has heard that my professional practices are in direct contradiction to the gospel. We spoke for some time, nothing satisfying him.

"Who has told you I was out of line?" I asked.

He would not say.

"Was it Elder Blanchard?" I asked.

"No," he said, "definitely not." Though under further scrutiny it became clear that he had been lying to me, that it was Blanchard.

"But it's my authority," he said. "He alerted me to a potential problem, but I'm the one investigating it. I'm the one making the decision."

Nonsense. A man you consider to have a direct conduit to God calls, tells you there's a problem, tells you what you should do about it. There's little chance, if you buy into the system, that you'll disagree.

It's the beginning of the end for me. It's just a question of time before I am forced out.

Nathan opening up a little.

What disturbs me is that though there seem to have been indications all along that Fochs was a predator, his standing in the Church largely blinded others to the signs. Even before he was provost, the fact that he was a clean-cut, regularly attending, apparently worthy member of the Church aided the will-to-blindness of everyone around him.

I was called in this morning again, before regular services, for a meeting with my provost. He again echoed his "love and support for me" but (always a but) "cannot allow me to stray any farther than I already have."

"It seems clear Elder Blanchard has been speaking to you," I suggested.

"Well," he said, "not precisely. I was going to speak to you anyway. Have you thought about what we discussed?"

I plunged through the charade, explained again with at least a pretense of patience what I do in my practice, why I don't resort to "Christianalysis," why I feel what I practice does not in the least contradict the teachings of the Church. As we talked, it became clear that either he had been given a copy of my Fochs papers or he had been told about them in detail. His questions were too knowing, too exact. When I called him on this, he denied it, said the Spirit must be guiding him.

It is a dirty game they play.

At the end, he still sat across the table, looking at me, all business in his suit, a faceless mannequin. His posture, attitude, gestures, made clear he had paid no attention to me and intended to pay none. This is the same man who told one of my patients whose husband was battering her that the "most important thing is that the family stay together," convincing the woman that she should drop charges and forget the abuse ever happened because the husband had promised never to do it again. Now she is dead.

"I'm sorry," he said, smiling. "I just can't see it. You must be deceiving yourself."

Then he had risen and was shaking my hand and guiding me toward the door. He was telling me that he was sure we could work this out, that we could come to an understanding, that if we continued to work together and I continued to pray and read my Scriptures, my heart would soften and I would embrace the truth fully. "Either you're on the team or you're against the team," he said, and smiled again. Then I was out in the hall and away from him.

It is a good religion, I told myself. There are good things about it, good values, even though there are problems as well, even though its leaders often choose to operate by coercion. The Church makes a lot of people happy. But it destroys people as well.

I sat in the pew and suffered through services, accepted the communion, making my appearance for the sake of my provost. From the podium, he smiled his encouragement.

Nathan is moving quickly forward in our daily meetings, though the long-term effects of Fochs's abuse have not even been glimpsed yet. Child abuse rewires the mind, often in subtle ways. It is impossible for me to predict, particularly in the early stages, how extensive the internal disruption has been.

He is old enough and has enough family support that I hope he will largely be able to absorb the abuse. He might survive it easier than, say, a five-year-old. Still, Nathan's life has been forever altered, and some of his potential has been shattered.

What I can surmise from Nathan's behavior and from what he has just now begun to tell me is that his abuse by Fochs went on for some time, that Fochs spent many months, and perhaps even years, gaining Nathan's trust and slowly manipulating the boy for his own purposes. There remains in Nathan an inappropriate amount of dependence on Fochs. Fochs, once he was provost, apparently took steps to convince Nathan that he was God. There seems to have been nothing random or unthought; rather, Fochs preyed on Nathan in cold blood. He spoke to Nathan at length and in increasingly graphic detail about sexual intercourse, claiming that since Nathan was "growing into a man" there were things he needed to know, but he would slide almost imperceptibly from speaking of heterosexual sex to what he told Nathan was "the sacred love between a child and a man," which, he claimed, was the most holy kind of love. Over an indeterminate period of time, Fochs suggested to Nathan that the temple rituals were tied to this sort of pedophilia, that all church members shared in it. Since access to the temple is restricted and the rituals cannot be discussed outside of the building itself, Fochs had a blank spot he could fill in with whatever image he wanted. Nathan could not know he was lying.

Soon Fochs began to caress the boy. When the caresses were responded to positively Fochs might slowly, over the next few weeks, do more. When his advances went too far and were again repulsed, he would step back and redouble the religious rhetoric he used to lower Nathan's defenses.

Fochs was expert at manipulating sacred texts to suit his own desires, an expert at parleying some of the teachings of the Church into a justification for his sins. The results for the children were a degree of ego extinction, loss of a clear sense of self, collapse of self-esteem, anxiety, anger, depression. Soul murder.

Church is hell. But if I stop going my clinic will fire me.

Provost again all over me. J. asking me, "Are you all right?" asking enough times that finally I told the truth and said no. He just stared, then looked uncomfortable.

Listening to the Fochs tapes again one detail stands out: the paper he said was hidden under the girl's tongue in his dream, the letters *B.H.* written on it. It never was reported in the newspaper. But that doesn't mean it wasn't in the girl's mouth.

On the way home I pulled into the mini-mart, climbed out, dialed the police from the pay telephone around the side of the building.

"I have a question about a murder case," I told the operator.

"Who shall I connect you with?"

I could see my perforated reflection, distorted on the curved, air-pocked sound barrier cupping the telephone. I watched myself. "It's not a question exactly," I said. "I may have some information."

The line clicked. When it was picked up again, a male voice said tersely, "What can you tell us?"

"I heard there was oil on the girl's head. Is that true?"

"Who told you that?"

"Another thing—was there anything under the girl's tongue?"

He was silent for some time. "What could possibly be under the tongue?" he asked.

"Two letters."

"What do you mean letters?"

"*B*," I said. "And *H*."

"Listen," said the voice. "No obligation. You can help us. Tell me where you are and we'll talk."

"I didn't do it," I heard myself saying. "But I know who did."

PART FOUR

FOCHS

CHAPTER 8

Holding Cell

I leave the office an hour early, time enough to take the bus not home but to the city complex. I introduce myself as clergy at the front desk, am led by a guard to the brother's holding cell. The guard opens the door, admits me, locks me in.

The boy is on the lower bunk, his back toward me.

"Want to talk?" I ask.

He turns slowly, just enough to see me, then turns back toward the wall.

"I thought it was your voice," he says. "Go away."

"I want to talk about your sister."

"I don't want to talk."

"She told me a lot about the two of you," I say. "I want to hear the truth from your own mouth."

"I didn't kill nobody," he says.

"I never said you did."

He pulls himself away from the wall, brings his feet flush to the floor. He looks at me, seems to look through me.

"Why are you here?" he asks. "Why, really?"

"I don't know," I say.

"You don't know?"

"I can't explain it," I say.

"Try," he says.

"No," I say. "Let's talk about you. Your sister died pregnant. The child was your child."

"I never touched her."

"She told me all about it."

"You're making it up. Besides, when did my sister talk to you?"

"She came in for an interview."

He smirks. "My sister never did that."

"What makes you think that?"

"We were close. She would have told me."

"She obviously didn't tell you everything," I say.

He shrugs.

"I want to hear the truth from your own lips," I say. "Admit it."

"None of your business."

"The truth is my business," I say. "The truth is God's business."

"Ask God, then," he says. "See if he tells you."

"Did you fuck her?" I ask.

"Pretty words from God's servant," he says.

"The kind of words someone like you understands. Did you?"

He lifts his feet onto the bed, rolls slowly back toward the wall.

"I can save you from yourself. I can save you from hell."

"I don't want to be saved from anything," he says.

"You are purchasing your own damnation."

"I didn't kill her."

"You might as well have. Every time you raped her, you were killing her."

"You don't know anything. I told you I never touched her."

"Everything is my business," I say. "Everything is God's province."

"God doesn't mean anything," he says, turning to look at me. "There's only you and me, Provost."

"And your sister."

"I didn't kill her," he says. "I had nothing to do with her death. I never touched her."

"We'll see," I say. "We'll see."

We stay staring at one another, the sun behind casting itself through the window mesh to mottle his skin. For a long time he says nothing, nor do I. Then he turns to face the wall again.

"You have as much potential as anyone else," I say. "Murderer or no. If you repent, you can one day be with God."

He shakes his head.

I look around at the bare cell walls, the toilet. "I have to leave," I say to the boy.

"Big mistake ever to have come," says the boy.

"I won't come again."

The boy shrugs.

I leave the cell, watch the door shut behind me. I look back at him, on the bunk, still facing the wall. He has hardened his heart. He doesn't believe in God. Even though he didn't kill her, he deserves whatever he gets.

CHAPTER 9

Approval

I am at the meeting house, late evening, conducting an interview with a member of my congregation to determine his worthiness to participate in the upper ordinances of the temple, when the telephone rings. It rings twice before being picked up in the secretary's office.

I go down the list of questions one after another, asking the man being interviewed to respond with a simple yes or no to each question. Through the door I can hear the secretary speaking, the sound of his voice but not his words.

"Nobody's perfect," I say as the man across from me wrings his hands, his face taut. "I am not perfect. You don't have to be perfect to partake of the blessings of the temple."

We go through the questions, the man hesitating before each question as if looking inward, and then responding faintly, "yes."

Filling out the temple approval form, I sign it. I have him sign it as well, tell him that he can still have the area rector sign it tonight if he hurries. I show him the door.

In the hallway, the chairs are empty, the hall dimly lit. I walk around the corner to the secretary's office, find Allen there.

"All done?" I ask. "No more appointments?"

"Somebody called for you," he says. He tears a scrap of paper from his planner and passes it to me. "Said it was urgent."

I look at the scrap, the telephone number, but do not recognize it. *Richard Foster.* I fold it into the skin of my palm.

"Who next?" I ask.

"Nobody," he says. "You're done."

I go into my office and shut the door. Taking up the telephone, I dial the number through. It rings four times, then is picked up. A child's voice.

"I am looking for Mr. Foster," I say.

"Can I say who is calling?"

"Can I speak to Richard Foster, please?"

"Who are you anyway?"

There is a sharp crack on the other end of the line, then the child is screaming, the sound slowly fading.

"Yes?" asks a new voice, a man's. "Richard Foster. Sorry about that."

"Mr. Foster," I say. "I had a message to call you."

"And you are?"

"Provost Fochs."

"Yes," he says. "Of course. Mr. Fochs, I work for the district attorney. Mr. Fochs, this has to do with the slaughtered girl."

"A tragedy. She was in my congregation."

"Her brother as well, no?"

"The whole family."

"It is only the brother who concerns us," he says. "We are considering prosecution. We would like you to testify to what the girl told you about him. The incest, I mean."

"He murdered her? You think he did it?"

"We think we have a case," he says. "We want to convict someone quickly to put the community at ease."

"I don't know," I say.

"With your testimony in the preliminary, the case should go to court. I think we can get him after that."

"I don't know."

"I'm not asking you, I'm telling you. We haven't got a case without you," he says. "Either you come willingly or we subpoena you. Just thought you should know.

On my way out, Allen stops me.

"The area rector is still in the building," he says. "He's doing temple approval interviews."

"Yes?"

"Your approval is expiring," he says, "if my records are correct."

I take the slip of paper out of my wallet. "So it is," I say.

"You won't be able to attend the special services," he says. "Just thought you would want to know."

I go back into the office, take out the approval book, write a slip up for myself. As provost I am called upon to testify to the worthiness of the members of my flock. Since I am a member of my own flock, I must determine my own worthiness. I interview myself and answer the questions. I read down the required list, question after question, answering them in my mind, and declare myself worthy of the higher blessings of the temple.

Signing the slip, I carry it down to the area offices. The door is open. Rector Bates is there, behind the desk, writing. I rap on the door frame, enter.

He looks up, looks down again.

"Provost," he says.

"Rector."

I take a seat across from him. In a moment he stops writing, sets his pen down beside the paper, rubs his palms. "What can I do for you, Provost?" he asks.

I remove the slip from my breast pocket and put it on the table before him.

"Approval renewal," I say.

"Of course," he says.

He picks up his pen, pulls the slip of paper closer. He brings the pen down, then lifts it away.

"I should go down the list of questions," he says. "But we've spoken recently. I assume you are worthy. Otherwise, you wouldn't even be here, right?"

"Correct," I say.

"We will assume you're worthy, Fochs," he says. "No need to answer the questions."

I nod.

"You are worthy, aren't you?"

"I wouldn't be here if I wasn't," I say. "Just like you said."

"That's good enough for me," he says. "Good boy."

He lines the pen up on the line, signs the slip.

"How have those women been treating you, Provost?"

"Women?"

"The ones who accused you of molesting their children."

"I haven't seen them."

"Been avoiding you, have they? Ashamed?" He hands me the slip. "Well, show them this," he says. "That should satisfy everybody."

"Thank you," I say.

"I know their kind of people," he says. "They have to be put in their place or they never stop yammering."

He opens the desk and removes an envelope, slit open along the edge. He shakes a letter out of it, hands the letter to me.

I unfold it, find it to be written by the women in question, addressed to an apostolic elder at church headquarters. It enumerates first my supposed abuse and then the sins of the area rector in protecting me. On the side of the page is scrawled an unsigned note, "Don't let this become a public issue." Rector Bates' name and address are written below in another hand.

"This letter is slanderous," I say.

"I'm in it now too," he says. "Next thing, they'll start approaching the newspapers if we don't stop them."

"How did you get this?"

"The Church sent it along," he says. "It's their policy to return everything like this to local leaders."

"They don't pay any attention?"

"I wouldn't say that. They go by the spirit. They trust us," he says. "We're called by God, aren't we?"

Nodding, I pass the letter back. He puts it into the envelope, then returns it to the desk.

"Call them in to speak with you," he says. "Deal with them gently, in the spirit of brotherly love. Command them to stop."

I lock the building and walk home, the sun long gone. I take the slow path, by the football field, skirting the woods where the girl was killed. I walk down the sidewalk until I reach my block.

At my corner, a man sits cross-legged on the sidewalk reading a book in the dim light of the street lamp. It is, I see as I approach, the Bible. His trousers are torn at the knees, most of the buttons of his shirt missing, his feet bare.

"Are you supposed to be here?" I ask.

He says nothing, doesn't lift his eyes from the page.

"I think it is time for you to be moving on," I say.

He lifts his head slowly, regards me steadily. "Sit down," he says.

"Do you want me to call the police?"

"Can it be you've forgotten me?"

I look at him closer, see his head razor cut and crusted with blood.

"Keeping an eye on you," Bloody-Head says. "Making certain you don't stray. Come on," he says. "I'll walk you home."

He reaches out his hand and I pull him up. He touches my shoulder lightly.

"You are worried about the women accusing you," he says. "I know. I can feel it."

"They're telling the truth."

"Only in a matter of speaking," he says. "What is truth, anyway?"

"They know what I did to their sons."

"Those boys provoked you," he says. "You are not to blame."

We walk until we reach my house. I can see the twins inside, their faces lit blue in the glow of the television.

"You aren't guilty, brother," he says.

"I don't know if I believe you."

"You have gone too far to stop believing in yourself now."

I start for the house.

"Wait," he says.

I keep walking. Somehow, he reaches the door before me.

"Suppose you are right," he says. "Suppose you are. It makes no difference. Whether you did it or not is not the issue. What is at issue is obedience."

"Obedience?"

"To fail to be obedient to your church leaders is to fail to be obedient to God. To speak evil of you is to speak evil of God."

He licks his lips, a cut on his forehead dark, glistening. "The area rector is doing the right thing. Whether you are worthy or not does not matter. Even if you lead people astray, they will be blessed for following you. And cursed for going against you."

I push past him, take the door handle in my hand.

"Invite me in to meet the family?" he says. "The wife?"

"No," I say. "Not here."

He shrugs. "Elsewhere, then. We'll all meet soon enough," he says. "Doesn't have to be today."

He slides into the bushes at the side of the house. I can see him between the hedge and the house wall, his body dim as if coming asunder. He waves to me, smiles, and then is gone.

CHAPTER 10

Confessions

A day later I am in Feshtig's office again. Usually there are more preliminaries, but today he sits across from me with his pencil poised. "Where would you like to begin?"

The two mothers are on my mind. I have been trying all night and all day to construct a method for dealing with them, for making certain they will not take the matter of their sons' abuse to the press. It would be foolish to say too much about the mothers to him, in case they do go to the press. I do the next best thing, the better thing: I manufacture a dream based on the truth.

I try to look nervous, reluctant. "With a dream," I say. "A disturbing one."

"Go ahead."

I begin to tell him about what I did to the boys in my office several months ago, pretending it was a dream. I change a few details, tinker with the boys' ages a little, but I keep the essential details the same.

As I tell it I find myself enjoying it again. Talking about it revivifies it. I have to keep reminding myself to watch my reactions, to try to keep my expressions and tone of voice those of shock and horror. It isn't easy.

Feshtig watches me carefully, without jotting anything on his pad for once. He is careful with his reactions as well, reserved even when I am recounting the best parts. But twice the corners of his eyes give him away. He can feel the power of what I have done, even though he will not believe I have done it. For him, it is still only a dream. This makes me feel even better.

I leave his office whistling under my breath, my burden lightened, my pleasure bursting. I am becoming a believer in the usefulness of therapy, but not in the way Feshtig would like. If I could, God knows, I would tell it all over again.

CHAPTER 11

Hearing

I sit in the back of the courtroom, my wife beside me, where I am less likely to be noticed.

"You are fidgety today," she says.

I am nervous, I admit.

The judge comes in. We rise, are told to be seated.

"There's the family," whispers my wife. "Right behind the defense."

"Where else would they be?"

"I was just saying."

"You didn't need to."

"Don't snap," she says. "Don't act like a child. What's the matter with you?"

"I shouldn't testify against the boy. It doesn't feel right."

"Pray about it," she says. "Just say a little prayer to beg God to help you."

Instead I look up at the judge, who is speaking. I look at the defense bench. The girl's brother is there, sullen, wearing a jacket and tie. The same ones he wears to church: he is the sort of boy who probably owns only one tie. His parents are behind, just across the other side of the gate.

"They are going to hate me," I say. "The family, I mean."

"You can't worry about what they'll think," she says. "You've got an obligation to the truth."

The judge is speaking and keeps speaking, I'm not sure how long. He pauses for a moment, starts off again. The prosecution stands up, delivers a speech, which I don't manage to follow, and then he sits down. The defense stands, argues to postpone the arraignment until bodily fluids tests arrive the following day.

"We'll hear the testimony," says the judge. "We will consider the test results when they arrive."

I see from the front of the court someone standing, waving.

"Who is it?" I ask.

"What?" my wife asks.

"That fellow waving."

She straightens herself in her chair, tugs down the hem of her skirt. She lifts herself slightly from the chair, peers past the heads in front of us.

"Nobody's waving," she says. "What's wrong with you?"

I keep watch but the gesture is not repeated, the man seeming to have sat down. The prosecution stands and says something about the brutality of a man who would rape and kill his own sister. The judge stares down, benevolent but hard, like God. It makes my breath go just watching him.

I stand and stumble out into the hall. I lean against the wall, outside the courtroom, taking deep breaths.

"What's the matter?" someone is asking. "Can I help you?"

My wife is beside me, touching my back. "Honey?" she asks. "What's wrong?"

She will not stand back, stays staring into my face.

"Some fresh air," I say. "Some air is all."

There is a sort of murmuring and my wife backs away, her face replaced by a man's legs.

"I'm a doctor," the legs say. "Can I help?"

"Just let me catch my breath."

The doctor tries to lift my head, but I will not let him lift it. He tries to draw me over to a bench, but I will not move.

"All the rest of you should go back in," he says. "You too, Mrs. Fochs. He needs some time alone to calm down."

I hear them leaving, my wife saying something comforting to me in parting.

"Take a deep breath," the doctor says.

"Leave me alone," I say.

"I can't do that," the doctor says.

He puts his hand on my face and jams two fingers up my nose, drags them up. It hurts. My head comes up with them.

"Jesus," I say.

"Is that any way to address a doctor?" he asks.

I try to get his fingers free and he hits me in the throat so I can't breathe. He sweeps his other arm around and over my neck, pulls me by the neck against his body, in a headlock, the fingers of his other hand still crammed up my nose.

"I want you to come with me," he says. "I don't want to have to break your neck."

He pulls me along and I go, shuffling my feet to keep up with him.

"Don't drag your feet," he says. "Pretend you can take human steps."

I try to step as he suggests and slip. He ends up dragging me by the neck into another room. Beyond his arm I can see tile on the floor and on some walls too.

He pulls me into a stall, forces me down so I'm looking into the toilet. Slowly he takes the fingers from my nose. They are streaked with blood and mucous. He flicks them, spattering the seat.

"I will release your neck in a moment so as to latch the stall door," he says. "Don't move."

I watch the blood drip from my nose, splash the water, diffuse.

"Okay," I say.

He lets go. I run my forearm under my nose, leaving a streak of blood near the wrist. I hear him latch the door.

"Sit down," he says.

"What?"

"You heard me."

I squat on the toilet. He takes some toilet paper off the roll, wads it, hands it to me.

"Your nose is bleeding," he says. "It's your own fault, of course. You should have come when I asked."

I hold the tissue up against my nose. He leans back against the door. "Well," he says. "Feeling better?"

"No."

"You are going to go through with this?"

"Through with what?"

"You know what," he says.

I look at the toilet paper in my hand, the blood on it, and press it back against my nostrils.

"I am doing the right thing."

He shakes his head. "You and I know the boy isn't guilty," he says.

"I don't know anything like that," I say.

"You killed the girl," he says. "There is no way around that fact. Are you going to let that boy be blamed for what you did? Who do you think you are, some kind of reverse Jesus, flitting about dispensing sin?"

"Who are you, talking like this?" I ask.

"I am a doctor."

"You're no doctor," I say.

"God or the Devil? You've got about three seconds. Choose."

I hear the door to the bathroom squeak open. "Fochs?" a voice asks. "You in there?"

The doctor moves into the front corner of the stall, puts his finger to his lips.

"Fochs?" the voice asks.

"Yes," I say. "I'm here."

The doctor grimaces, rolls his eyes.

A knocking comes on the stall, black leather boots show under the door. "Fochs?" the voice asks.

"Just a minute," I say. "I'm coming out."

I see fingers fold over the top of the stall door, above the doctor's head. The whole stall shakes and creaks, the boots lift off the ground. A bald, bloody head rises above the stall door, eyes just barely cresting over. The doctor shrivels into his corner.

"What are you doing?" Bloody-Head says to me. "Your pants aren't even off."

"I'm coming," I say.

I stand up, reach for the door handle tentatively, my eyes on the doctor. He watches me but does not move. I open the door against him, as far as it will go, until it is forcing him into the wall, then squeeze my way out.

"You're all right?" asks Bloody-Head.

"I'm glad to see you," I say.

"Of course you are," he says. "No second thoughts?"

"None."

He pats my shoulder twice. "Good boy," he says.

He goes back into the court, me following. He opens the door and the whole court peers up at us, at me. Pushing me in next to my wife, he keeps walking down the aisle.

"Sir," the judge says, looking to me, "we are conducting a hearing here."

I nod my head, smile, sit down. A few people stay for a time looking back over their shoulders at me, then slowly turn to face front.

"You should enter with more dignity," my wife says.

"What did I do?"

She just shakes her head.

The bloody-headed man has kept walking and now stands before the witness box. Nobody is looking at him. He takes the fat, bald witness currently in the box by the lapels, drags him out of the chair and over the edge of the box, dropping him onto the floor of the court. The fat man says nothing, attempts to look at the judge who is speaking to him, then at the prosecution lawyer.

The bloody-headed man heaves the fat man onto his shoulder, staggering under his weight.

"Could you see who the boy was in your yard?" asks the prosecution.

The fat man opens his mouth like a fish, closes it. Bloody-Head staggers with him to the side of the room, grunting. The fat man begins to lift his head and his arm. He points at the boy, the veins standing out over all his face. The bloody-headed man throws him out the open window, closes the window tightly behind him.

He dusts his hands off, takes his place in the witness box.

"Was that bastard," Bloody-Head says, assuming a contrived rural accent. "That one over right there."

"Which one?" asks the prosecution.

"The one with the shit-colored hair."

People in the court laugh. The bloody-headed man smiles, the judge smiles as well.

"Could you point the boy out again?"

I wait for the defense to object, but they do not.

The bloody-headed man lifts his finger, points to the girl's brother.

"What was he doing?" the prosecution asks.

"He was lewd, like I never seen it before."

"Could you tell the court how he was lewd?"

The bloody-headed man looks around. "Got some ladies present," he says.

"It doesn't matter," says the prosecution. "Tell us."

Bloody-Head rises up in the box. He pantomimes for the court what he says the boy did to himself. The court laughs.

"Why are they laughing?" I whisper.

"Oh, he's a harmless old lout," my wife says.

"He was just whipping it around," Bloody-Head says. "And on my property too. Private property. By God, I wanted to sell the land after what he spilled there."

There is a noise behind me. I turn and see the doctor there, holding the door open slightly, his head back between his shoulders as if he is afraid of being struck.

"You're a sick man," he says, stretching his hand toward me. "Come with me."

"Don't go with him!" shouts Bloody-Head. "He's the Devil!"

"Don't listen to him," says the doctor. "I'm not the Devil. He's the Devil."

"Judge, I'm done with my testimony," says the bloody-headed man in his usual voice. "Can I step down?"

"Can't you see what you are doing here is wrong?" asks the doctor.

"God wants me to do it," I say.

"Defense?" queries the judge.

"You tell him, Fochs!" yells Bloody-Head.

The defense lawyer nods. "You may step down," says the judge.

"You have sold your soul, Fochs," says the doctor.

Bloody-Head rushes down the aisle and slams into the door, pushing the doctor out. He returns brushing his hands. Climbing onto the judge's desk, he leans down to fish a key from the judge's pocket, then returns to the door.

"Want me to lock him out?" he asks.

"Yes," I say.

"Yes," he says, turning the key. "Leave it to me."

"Thank you," I say.

"I am the one who loves you," he says.

"And God," I say.

"Yes," he says. "Why not? Go ahead and testify."

I realize the judge is staring at me. I stand slowly, make my way to the front of the court, climb into the witness box.

"It's you," the judge says. "The disturbance."

"Yes," I say. "I'm sorry."

"I don't believe you took the oath," he says.

"The oath?"

"You need to take the oath before you step into the box," says the judge.

"Oh," I say. "Of course."

I stand up and step down, move to one side.

"Raise your hand," says Bloody-Head, from behind the Bible. I raise it.

"Do you swear to tell the truth, the whole truth, and nothing but the truth, so help you God?" Bloody-Head winks at me. "Say yes," he says. "Don't try to explain."

"I do," I say.

"You're not getting married, Fochs," says Bloody-Head. "Yes will do."

"Take your place," says the judge.

Bloody-Head goes to the prosecution lawyer, whispers into his ear. The man listens, nods. He stands, crawls underneath the table. Bloody-Head steps forward.

"I have just a few questions," he says.

"Okay," I say.

"You were acquainted with the girl who was killed?" he asks.

"Yes."

"How did you know her?"

"I was her spiritual leader."

"In what sense?"

"I was the minister of the congregation she attended. The Corporation of the Blood of the Lamb. She consulted me about moral difficulties she was having."

"What sorts of moral difficulties?"

"She had serious moral challenges facing her."

Bloody-Head walks around a little.

"Do you know the defendant?"

I say that I do.

"How do you know him?"

"He is in the congregation as well. The deceased's sister."

"Brother, you mean."

"Brother. Of course."

"Did the brother ever say anything to you about the sister?"

"I never met with the sister."

"The brother, you mean."

"Yes, of course. I never met with the brother."

Bloody-Head comes close to the box, leans toward me.

"Slow down. Think about what you are saying," he says. "God knows you want to do the right thing. Now do it."

I nod. I take a deep breath. He steps back.

Through the side window I see the doctor waving his hands back and forth.

"Did you ever meet with the sister, Mr. Fochs?"

"The brother, you mean," I say.

"No, godammit," he says. "I mean what I say."

"The sister," I say. "Yes, I have met with the sister," I say.

"How many times?" he asks.

"Just once," I say.

He comes closer to the bench. "I thought we went over this. You should have said two or three times," he says.

"Should I say it now?"

"Excuse me?" says the judge.

"No," says the bloody-headed man. "You can't change the story now."

"Did you say something?" the judge asks me.

"I wasn't saying anything."

The doctor is outside the window, pounding. His eyes are wide. I do not know how he has managed to climb up there.

"Did she say anything to you at that time about her brother?"

"I never met with the brother."

"Fuck the brother!" Bloody-Head yells. I flinch, but nobody else moves.

"What did she say?"

"That she was having sexual relations with her own brother."

The whole court seems to moan.

"What do you mean by sexual relations?" he says.

"Intercourse," I say. "Fornication."

"Sex?"

"Yes," I say.

"And what was the result?"

"She was made pregnant."

"She was impregnated by her own brother?"

"Yes, by her brother."

"That brother over there?"

"Yes," I say. "Over there."

"Incest, you mean?"

"That is what she said."

"Did she say anything else?"

"She said she was frightened of her brother."

"Why?"

"She worried what he would do if he found out she was pregnant."

"Did she say what she thought he would do?"

"No," I say.

He looks at me hard.

"Did she say what she thought he would do?" he asks, louder.

"I can't remember," I say.

"Speak up," says the judge.

"I cannot remember," I say.

"You are ruining this," Bloody-Head hisses. "I thought you were ready for a little responsibility. But you aren't ready for anything."

"I'm sorry." I truly am.

"If you were really sorry, you would invite me to take a turn in your life," Bloody-Head says. "You would tell me you want me to take your place."

"Take it," I say.

"What?" asks the judge. "Sorry?"

"Step down," Bloody-Head says.

I climb down, go down the aisle back to my seat with my wife. She will not look at me, does not seem to know I am there. I watch Bloody-Head first speak from the floor, then step into the witness box, then speak from the floor, playing both prosecution and witness. My wife is nodding, smiling.

"That's showing them," she whispers.

Then the people in the court are on their feet, shouting, the judge raps the gavel. The court quiets down, the people slowly return to their seats.

The judge points his gavel at Bloody-Head, sitting in the witness box.

"One more time, Fochs," he says. "Just one more. I am warning you."

Bloody-Head nods, slowly smiles.

"Excuse me," I say. "I am Fochs."

I stand up. "Excuse me," I say. "I don't mean to interrupt. He is not Fochs. Fochs is me."

The judge does not even turn his head. The bloody-headed man just smiles, winks at me, keeps talking.

I close my eyes and when I open them I am in the front. The whole court is standing, moving out.

"You were wonderful, honey," says my wife.

Other people are shaking my hand and patting me on the shoulder, congratulating me. I see the accused and his family flash past, looking deliberately away. Then Bloody-Head is there, shaking my hand.

"Well done," he says. "That last bit of testimony sealed it."

"Did it?" I ask.

"Don't underestimate yourself," he says. "Especially when you have the right friends."

He leans in closer, whispers in my ear. "You've been meeting with the psychoanalyst," he says. "Does that make you feel better?"

I shrug. "I think so," I say.

"Be careful what you say," he says. "It only takes one slip."

He turns, sees my wife.

"Is this your wife?" he asks. "Aren't you going to introduce me?"

"My wife," I say.

"Hello," my wife says.

"Charmed," he says. "A good friend of your husband's, Mrs. Fochs. A great admirer as well. You have children?"

"Four," my wife says. "Two girls, two boys."

"Lovely," he says. "Perhaps I will meet them sometime."

"Perhaps we can have you over for dinner," she says.

"No!" I say. They both look at me. "Not now, I mean," I say. "Too busy."

"What a shame," says my wife. "Perhaps some other time," she says. "Soon."

"Soon, then," he says.

"I don't know your name," says my wife.

"I am a friend of your husband," he says. "A good friend."

"That's true," I say.

"He owes me a lot," he says. "And I owe him my existence." He pats me on the shoulder. "I need to speak to your husband privately," he says. "Can you excuse us a moment?"

She nods, takes a few steps back.

"We've won," I say.

"No," he says. "As soon as they have the results of the fluids tests, they'll know it wasn't him. We've just bought a few days."

"But they don't know it's me."

He shrugs. "They'll gather a list of subjects. Narrow the pool by blood typing, narrow further by selecting a few from that pool for DNA testing. You probably won't be on the list, but you can never be certain. Of course," he says, "I could help you."

"How?"

"Oh, I don't know," he says. "I'm a man of many talents. If I do help, I would want something from you in return."

"What do you want?"

"I don't know," he says. "What do you have to offer?"

CHAPTER 12

Church

I am lying down, my wife is stripping off her hose. She leaves them beside the bed, the two legs coiled into one another.

She comes closer, turns away from me, sits on the edge of the bed.

"Unzip me?" she asks.

I draw the zipper down and watch the fabric part, spread wide. I see her spine seamed in pale knots through the shallow flesh. She stands, pulls her sleeves off her elbows, lets them fall so that the top of her dress hangs deflated around her waist, her bra revealed.

"Who was that man?" she asks.

"What man?"

She parts her bra at the back and rolling her shoulders shrugs it off. She plucks at the fabric beneath her breasts, where it has stuck to her skin, her nipples dark through the white mesh.

"The attorney in court the other day," she says. "The one who questioned you on the stand."

"Him?" I ask. "A friend of mine."

"A good friend?"

"Sure, why not?"

She climbs into bed next to me. She moves beneath the covers, smoothes them over her belly.

"Why haven't I heard of him before?" she wants to know.

"I don't know. Just didn't think of it."

"Didn't think of it? He said you saved his life."

I shrug. "He didn't say that exactly. I don't remember what he said. I don't know what he meant by that," I say. "Just prosecutor. I helped him on a project once. Maybe that's all he means."

"What sort of project?"

"Hell, I can't remember. Nothing special."

"I was just asking," she says. "Don't curse."

She turns over and away from me. I reach over and turn off the light.

"No need to snap," she says.

I grunt.

"Something is wrong with you," she says. "I know you. Something is wrong."

"Nothing is wrong," I say. "Leave me alone."

She stays quiet for a while, conspicuously not moving.

"I don't want him in our house," I say. "I hardly know the fellow. We won't invite him over."

"Okay," she says.

Later, when I am almost asleep, she says, "Something is the matter with you."

"Nothing is the matter," I say. "Open your thick skull and listen for once."

"I don't want to hear you talk like that," she says. "I want the truth."

There is no way I am going to tell her the truth.

"I want the truth," she says again. "Do you hear me?"

"Go to sleep," I say. "I am too tired for truth. We'll talk in the morning."

"Promise?"

"Promise."

...

I get up early and leave before my wife wakes. I walk to the church and unlock the doors. Entering my office, I shut the door, put my head on the desk, sleep.

My two counselors wake me when they arrive. I slog through our Sunday morning meeting, hardly aware. The secretary reminds me that I am scheduled both to conduct and present the second address in the main service today. I haven't prepared anything.

Before Sunday school convenes, I walk out to the steps, where I wait until my wife's car pulls up. I walk down and open the back door, take my youngest out of her car seat. The twins are already out and rushing up the stairs, my eldest following serenely after, pretending she is grown.

"Take her to the nursery," my wife says.

"No," I say. "I can't take her."

"It's your turn to take her," she says.

"I'm sorry, I have to prepare my address."

"This always happens," she says. "Every week. I guess I should expect it from you by now."

"Don't be like that," I say. "I can resign. You don't want me to be the provost? You don't want me to serve the Lord?"

"No," she says. "It isn't that."

I hold our youngest at arm's length, toward my wife. The child tries to turn around in my arms to face me. My wife looks down at her feet, puts her hands behind her back.

"Is it going to kill you to take her?" she asks.

"It is not only the address," I suggest. "It is the two women as well. The ones harassing me."

She hesitates, then takes the baby.

"We never talked," she says.

I shrug. I have nothing to say.

I am sitting down in my church office, writing the address when the two women arrive.

"Sit down," I say. "Leave the door ajar, please."

They sit coolly on the far side of the room, their backs straight, their legs crossed at the knees. Women are like dogs, I think. Get them alone and give them a snack and they can be nice enough. Get them together and they develop a pack mentality.

I pass the letter they have written to the apostolic elder across the table to them.

"This has come to my attention."

They glance furtively at one another.

"Nobody likes someone who can't pull with the team. People who write letters like this lose the faith."

"We are worthy members," one says. "We go to meetings, we pay our tithing, we obey all the commandments."

"Unlike someone else in this room," says the second, snidely. She is the worst of the two. The troublemaker.

"Whatever you think I am," I say, "it is wrong for you to be disobedient to your spiritual leaders. Those who malign their spiritual leaders are not for the Church, and whoever is not for the Church is against it. You are against it."

They become irate, but I pay them little heed. I tell them what they need to hear by yelling louder than them.

"God will discipline you!" I yell. "Both of you!"

They shout some more, all meaningless, and then storm out.

I take out my handkerchief and wipe my forehead. There are, I realize, a few people grouped around the office door, looking in.

"Will you please close the door?" I ask. Then I get up and close it myself.

I start to work on my address again, listening to the voices murmur on the other side of the door. I will speak on obedience, for it has become clear to me that in matters of obedience some of my congregation are severely lacking.

The bell marking the midway point of Sunday school rings. I take a few more notes and then stand. I open the door. A few people are still there, grouped around the door, speaking. They fall silent as the door opens.

"You should be studying the Scriptures," I say. "All of you. You are going to be late."

They file reluctantly away. I return to my office. I open the Holy Scriptures, mark some passages I might quote.

I am in the midst of communing with the holy and revealed word when the door opens and two dark-suited gentlemen enter.

"Can I help you?" I ask.

"We don't mean to disturb you," says one. "But we must speak with you."

"I would be happy to meet with you," I say, "but I'm in a rush right now. Perhaps we can do this later?"

"No," the second says. "We must do this now."

They make their way in, shutting the door behind them. They sit down.

"We've been sent to ask you some questions," says the first.

"Questions?" I ask. "What right have you to question me?"

"We're here to assess your performance." The other has taken a pad of paper and a pencil from his pocket and is scribbling on the pad.

"I don't understand."

"No," the second man says. "We are the ones who don't understand. Thus, the questions."

"First things first," says the first man. He clears his throat. "Do you have any signs or tokens?"

"I don't know what kind of game this is."

"He doesn't have any."

"I have them," I say. "I hold them sacred."

"You haven't shared them? You've held them sacred, you claim?"

"What I do is none of your business. Who do you think you are?"

"We don't write the questions," says the second. "We just ask them. Don't blame us."

"We're not asking about your personal life," says the first. "Only if you've held your covenants sacred."

"That is not my personal life?"

"It is much grander than your personal life," he says.

"Do you perform the sacred rites of the temple outside of the temple itself?" asks the second.

"What?"

"Do you?" he asks.

"Absolutely not," I say.

"Have you taken secret wives and thereby violated the new and everlasting covenant of marriage?"

"Let me ask the questions," the first says. He turns to me. "Have you ever practiced bigamy?"

"One wife is more than enough for me to handle," I say.

They just look at each other.

"Are you saying you are not living up to your marriage obligations?" says one.

"Are you saying that if the Lord asked you to take a second wife, you'd have difficulty following the Lord's command?" says the other.

"No," I say. "I'm not saying that at all."

"What are you saying?" asks the second. "Perhaps you should think before you speak."

"I'm saying I am willing to serve the Lord," I say. "Heart and soul."

"That was not what you said."

"I don't know what it sounded like I was saying, but that was what I was saying. Write it down."

"I will write down things as I hear them. Not what you tell me to write down."

"Let's talk some more," says the first man. "There is more left to ask."

"I don't want to talk anymore," I say. "I'm busy. I don't even know who you are. I don't have to take this from you."

"Who's taking what?"

"Just a few more questions. We'll go away after that."

I calm down. I show these gentlemen the kind of self-control the Lord's anointed have, to teach them a lesson.

"Go ahead," I say. "I will indulge you."

"I want to ask about the girl."

"What girl?"

"The one you killed."

"I don't know who you mean."

"That's what this is all about," says the second. "It all comes down to the girl."

"I won't answer anything about any girl," I say.

"We can't force you, but it will be better for you to tell us."

"You cannot hide from God," says the other.

"I love God," I say. "God is the last one I'd try to hide from."

They look at each other, break out in peals of laughter.

"What?" I ask. "What is it?"

They wipe their eyes.

"What about the law of chastity?" says the first.

"What about it?" I say.

"Do you live it?"

"I am one of its adherents," I say, "in my own way."

"What way is that?" says the second.

"You keep out of this," the first says to him. "You only make this worse." He turns to me. "We are merely trying to obtain a clear picture of how things are," he says. "Personally, we don't care. We're only messengers."

"Messengers?"

He and the other man look at each other, smirk.

"Back to the matter at hand. The law of chastity."

"I answered that," I say.

"What did you mean, in your own way?" he asks.

"I mean I live it," I say. "I am chaste."

"Why in your own way?" the second asks. "What about the girl?"

"No," I say. "I won't speak about her anymore."

"All right, that's fine."

"We can help you. Don't you want help?"

"I don't need help from anybody," I say.

"What about God?"

"Except God," I say. "I was forgetting God."

"That's been your problem all along."

"You obey the commandments, Fochs?" says the first.

"I obey them," I say.

"In your own way?" says the second.

The first one coughs, looks down at the floor.

"What about *Thou shall not kill*?" he asks.

"That one I certainly obey," I say.

"You obey that?" asks the second, shaking his head.

"I am a good and faithful servant."

"I can write that down?" asks the second.

I shrug. "Sure," I say. "It's the truth, isn't it?"

"Whatever you say," says the second man.

"Get out."

"One more question," he says.

"I am through with questions. No more questions."

"One more question," he says, standing.

He reaches into his pocket, removes a photograph, an older one. The edges are cut wavy, like the edges of a paper plate, the surface of the image itself cracked. He puts it on the desk.

"Do you know what this is?" he asks. "Do you recognize the face?"

I examine the photograph. It is a man wearing a business suit, carrying a valise, his hair neatly parted down the center line of his head and slicked down the sides. I do not recognize him at first, then see in him, under the hair, the bloody-headed man.

I look up and know I have seen the two men before, on the bus chasing the bloody-headed man, then again dragging him away during the girl's funeral.

"Well?" they ask.

I take the notes for my talk and fold them in half, slipping them inside my Scriptures. I get up from my chair.

"We know you know him," says the second. "We know. All we need to know is how well."

"Are the two of you friends?" asks the first. "Would you call yourself close?"

"God help you," says the second.

"Do you even know who he is?" asks the first.

"Are you collaborating with him? God help you if you are."

I push by them.

"I won't have you in my church!" I shout.

"No, you wouldn't want us here, would you?"

"We're going," says the first. "Don't worry."

"Tell your buddy hello," says the second. "Say hello from us."

And then they are gone.

I am shaking hands with all of the congregation, inquiring after their health, showing my love and concern, trying to make it through the crowded lobby into the chapel.

I can see, at the inner doors, holding them open for me, the bloody-headed man. He is smiling.

I can see, at the far side of the foyer, the two women who want to decry me, surrounded by their cronies, three or four other unpleasant women, whose names I immediately note on the card in my shirt pocket.

I can see, beside the outer doors, the two men in suits who have questioned me.

The press of them is all around me.

And here is God, in his awful glory, come streaming down through the firmament to embrace me.

CHAPTER 13

Collapse

"Do you want anything?" my wife's voice is asking.

I swallow but do not open my eyes. I try to get up but find I cannot. Someone is brushing their hand across my face. I try to open my eyes but find they will not open.

"Someone is holding down my eyelids," I say. My voice sounds blurred, incomplete. I do not know how much I have actually managed to say.

"Don't speak," my wife says. "Don't try."

I flutter my eyelids. They will not open.

"No," she says. "Please."

I hear her speak further, then fade away. A door opens and shuts. My body refuses to be my body. I lie still.

I feel some weight against my kneecap, and then on one side of my chest. I get my eyes cracked open enough to see Bloody-Head above me, riding my body, leaning his face in. He presses his face against mine, his lips against my lips. I try to turn my head to one side but he brings his hands up, holds my head still. He pushes his tongue into my mouth, runs it across my teeth. He brings his thumbs away from my ears, turns them downward to rest on my throat just beneath the chin. He pushes down until all air is blocked.

"You are doing great now," he says. "Keep it up."

He eases his thumbs off. I gasp.

"Where did you learn to kiss?" he asks. "Can't you do better than that?"

He pushes the tips of his thumbs in at the backs of the cheeks, just behind the teeth, until my jaw loosens and draws slightly open. He pushes his tongue through my teeth, strokes the roof of my mouth, leaves his tongue pushing against the back of my throat, wriggling.

I bite down hard, feel the blood slick its way down my throat, choking me. By the time I realize he is pushing up on my chin with his fist, helping me to bite the tongue off, it is too late to stop.

He pulls his head away, the forepart of his tongue tearing free behind my teeth, the last bits stringing through his gums. He keeps holding my chin shut.

"Swallow it," he says, blood dripping from his lips, his voice clear despite the missing portion of his tongue.

I am shaking my head, trying to get it away. The slit tongue slips around my mouth, wriggling.

"Swallow," he says.

He brings his head down and begins to massage my throat with his lips. He turns his head sideways and brings his teeth against either side of my windpipe, bites down until I can no longer breathe.

And then lets go.

"You can't know all you've done for me," he says. "Not truly." He says, "Swallow or I will kill you."

I awake in my bed, the taste in my mouth gone, my body sweat drenched and awkward. I try to move, find that the room springs up around me in slow motion.

"Darling," my wife says. "Lie down."

I let her push my head softly back onto the cushions. She stands and leaves, her heels ringing against the parquet until she reaches the carpeting of the hall. I stay staring at the ceiling, tracing the cracks to the light and back. I close my eyes, see the dull afterimages behind my lids.

There is the sound of my wife's footsteps returning, coming to the side of the bed. The sound of her breathing, a slight stir of the air.

"Drink this."

She puts her hand under my neck, lifts my head, puts something cold against my lips. I drink feebly, feel the water trickle from the sides of my mouth, until the cup is taken away.

"How do you feel?" she asks.

"What was it?"

"I don't know," she says. "You fell down with your muscles locked up. A seizure of some sort."

"I don't understand."

"Neither do I."

I open my eyes long enough to see her face, the soft lines of it, the way she leans over me as she does the children when they are sick. She stays that way until she notices I am looking at her, then pulls herself back, folds her arms.

"There is something I would like to talk about when you feel better," she says.

"What?"

"Not now. You need to rest."

"I am feeling a little better," I suggest.

She stays looking at me, clutching herself in her arms, blowing air out.

"Don't bring it up if you aren't going to talk," I say.

"Your secretary Allen came to me at church, asked me if we'd managed to get the telephone line fixed. I didn't know what he was talking about. He said you had been having problems with it when you had called him the night the girl died. 'You mean when you called us,' I said to him, 'to tell him about his appointment that night.' 'Appointment?' he said. 'There was no appointment that night. The schedule was free.'"

She stops talking, looks at me. "I want to know what that is all about," she says.

I just shake my head.

"Where did you go that night?"

"I went out," I say. "Nothing serious."

"Where?"

"I'm exhausted. We'll talk it over later."

"No," she says. "Now."

I close my eyes, keep them closed. She reaches out, touches me.

"Trust me," I say.

"If I find out you had anything at all to do with that girl's death . . ." she says. I just lie there, ignoring the rest of it, already thinking through what I can tell her.

"Those two boys," she says. "I know you did that."

"What boys?"

"You know who," she says. "The ones whose mothers have been after you. I know what you did. I can forgive that as a slip if you swear never to do it again."

"What did I do?"

"Don't make me say it," she says. "If I have to face it, I don't think I can forgive you."

I just close my eyes.

"We will think of that as a slip," she says. "A reversion. Your brother told me all about you when we were getting married. I thought you'd changed, that you'd given all that up when you grew up. I didn't want to believe it, but still I knew. So it was my fault."

I am willing to let her take whatever blame she chooses. I will accept her collaboration.

"But you can't do it anymore," she says. "Promise me you won't do it again."

What do I have to lose? Of course I promise her.

"Swear it before God."

I swear without hesitation. This seems to satisfy her. She leaves me alone.

"Do you love me?" I ask.

"I don't know," she says. She lifts our youngest out of the high chair, puts her into the crib.

"I love you," I say. "I love you more than anything."

"I guess I do," she says wearily. "I'm still with you, aren't I?"

"You've done the right thing," I say.

I come close to kiss her, but she won't face me. I go back to the table, eat the scraps of toast the children have left scattered. I carry the plates over to the counter, past it to the sink.

"Besides," she says, "the children need a father."

"I'll be a good father to them."

I go upstairs and get my briefcase, come down again.

"We'll be together now and we'll be together in heaven," I tell her. "We'll be together always."

"Not heaven. Not after what you did to those boys," she says.

"Nonsense," I say. "It will work out. You'll see."

When I get to the office, I telephone the area rector. I tell him about the women on Sunday, about how they have been causing trouble and leading others astray. I tell him that they might go to the press and cause the Church a great deal of trouble. He perks right up.

"We don't want anything to happen that could damage the Church's name," he says.

"No," I say.

"When will they go to the press?"

"I don't know. We have a few days maybe."

"We'll talk to them. We'll resolve the matter as quickly as possible. We'll catch them spinning so fast they won't know what hit them."

CHAPTER 14

Final Session

I take Bloody-Head's warning about revealing too much at therapy to heart. Before the session with Feshtig, I spend twenty minutes in the parking lot in my car, considering what I will say this time. I search for something that will please me even more than last week's story about my chastening of the boys, something to keep him off balance, something new.

The only thing that will do is the murder.

But it would be a mistake to speak of the murder. It is too close, too open to investigation.

Though, if I tell it as a dream . . .

No, it is too much of a risk.

Still, it is what I want to talk about.

"Feeling lucky?" asks Bloody-Head.

"I don't know," I say.

"Tell if you want," he says. "Take a few chances. But don't say I didn't warn you."

"We've been making a great deal of progress," suggests Feshtig.

"Yes," I say. "We really have."

"How have your dreams been?"

"They haven't stopped, if that's what you mean."

"Are they still as frequent?"

I shrug. "A little less."

He sits staring at me until I begin to talk, constructing a new dream on the fly. I describe Bloody-Head's face to him, his nicks and cuts, say that he was the one who killed the girl.

"In the dream, did you have a name for him?"

"He doesn't have a name."

"Did you call him anything?"

I consider whether I dare tell him the truth, then figure it can't hurt. "Sure," I say. "Bloody-Head."

"Why?"

"Because he was a bloody head."

"Didn't he have a body?"

I think a moment, guess at what he wants to hear. "I was his body," I suggest.

"He was your head?"

"My head was my head. He was extra."

"He was a part of you?"

"He wasn't a part of me, he was attached to me."

"Why did he have a bloody head?"

"How should I know? I just dreamed it."

"You dreamed he engineered the murder of the girl?"

Yes, I am going to say, but when I look up I see Bloody-Head behind Feshtig, shaking his head no.

I avoid the question. I begin describing the murder as it might have been if I had stumbled across it, the scene from the outside, after the murder. I try to lead him away, but he keeps drawing things back to the bloody-headed man. Bloody-Head himself just stays standing behind him, shaking his head, arms crossed.

"How did his head become bloody?"

"I don't know."

"Did you feel the cuts were purposeful or accidental?"

I can't figure out why he wants to know this, how he'll interpret what I'll say. "I don't know," I say in some confusion. "Out of necessity maybe."

He makes a note. Behind him, Bloody-Head is frowning. I look down, keep my head down, so I won't have to look at him.

"In the dream, he didn't seem all bad," I suggest.

"No?"

I glance up in time to see Bloody-Head draw his finger across his throat.

Feshtig turns around in his chair and stares through Bloody-Head, then turns back to me. I start to get nervous.

"What did you mean when you said he wasn't all bad?"

I do not need to look up to know that Bloody-Head is waving his hands, shaking his head. I stumble through a few responses and then clamp down, bide my time until the session runs out.

When I open the door, Bloody-Head is in the car.

"Brother," he says, "don't go back."

"Why not?"

"You've given too much away."

"I've changed things," I say.

"He's smarter than you think. He's given you enough relief that you'll sleep easy. Be satisfied with that."

I start the car.

"Do you hear me?" he asks.

"I heard you," I say. "I have a question of my own: who are you?"

"Who am I?"

"Are you Jesus?"

"Jesus? What do you think?"

I think about it a while. "Yes," I say. "I think you are."

He smiles. I take this as confirmation.

"I'll stop then," I say. "I won't go back. Anything for Jesus."

CHAPTER 15

Court

We spring it on them. We hand deliver to each boy's mother the letter indicating that their church court will be held the evening of the following day. We telephone each member of the Area Council, making arrangements for substitutes for the several councilors who will be unavailable.

Before the court begins, the area rector meets with the Area Council, explains to them that the two women simply want to defame the Corporation of the Blood of the Lamb. He tells them that to do this they have constructed elaborate lies about me, their provost.

"The accusations they will raise against this good brother are false," says the area rector. "I testify to you he is innocent."

The women arrive surrounded by their supporters, who have decided to hold vigil until the court is concluded. They are all forced to wait outside the building, in the rain. The area rector sends each of the area councilors out one by one, has them write down the name of anyone they recognize in the group. The press is there as well, and all the television stations, except the one owned by the Church.

Rector Bates himself is nervous. He stays inside the Area Council room with me, licking his lips.

"These women," he says. "No respect for authority. They delight in embarrassing the Church."

He tells this to each of the area councilors as they enter. Later, we bring the two women in and have them sit at the far end of the table, the sixteen of us men packed together as far away from them as possible.

The area rector begins by introducing everyone present to the women. He is all smiles.

"The church Disciplinary Council is not a court," he tells the women. "This is a council of love. We are not here to punish you. We are here to do what is best for you. We love you deeply." He reaches down to the desk and reads off the paper. "You have been accused of unchristianlike conduct and disobedience to your leaders. How do you plead?"

"Since when is disobeying a corrupt leader grounds for a court?" the brunette asks.

"Obedience to authority is the law upon which all other laws are predicated," says Rector Bates.

"You shouldn't obey when your leaders tell you to do something you know to be wrong," the brunette says.

"If you follow their counsel—even if you believe you are being asked to do something wrong—you will be blessed. In any case, Provost Fochs did not ask you to do something wrong. You have accused Provost Fochs of crimes he did not commit. You have made him suffer greatly."

"Did not commit?" says the brunette.

"This is not a council for Fochs," says the area rector. "This is a trial for you. Not another word about Fochs."

Bates gets up and starts to pace at the far end of the table, behind the other men.

"Shouldn't we be tried separately?" the blond asks.

"First of all," says Rector Bates, "it doesn't have to happen that way. We can examine you both at once since your crimes are the same. Second, this is not a court at all but a council of love. You aren't being tried. Now," he says. "I want you both to admit you wrongly accused Fochs, that you lied."

The two women get indignant about this. The area rector points to the clerk and tells him to make a note of their attitudes. The women become silent and sullen.

"Do you want to be in the Church or not?" Rector Bates asks them.

Yes, they say, they do.

"Let me say it again," he says. "Will you admit to lying?"

"No," says the brunette, and then, more reluctantly, the blond.

"I am not surprised," he says. "Not at all." He walks around a little bit, seeming to enjoy himself. "I want to ask another question," he says. "In the letter we mailed to you, we asked you not to speak about the disciplinary process to reporters. Why did you notify the press that you were meeting with the Disciplinary Council?"

"We didn't," says the blond. "Someone else called them."

"No," says the area rector. "That can't be true. No councilor would dare notify the press. It must have been you. That you called the press indicates an unwillingness to repent."

"We called no one."

"You should stop lying. You should stop attacking the Lord."

"We never attacked the Lord."

"To attack the Church is the same as attacking the Lord."

There are more arguments, blunt attempts by the area rector to get the women to admit they are lying. He has already made his decision—either they get in line with him or he will shake himself free of them. I stay quiet, watching it all, feeling that I am somewhere else.

After a few hours of bashing heads and of what he calls their "unrepentant tears," the area rector gives up on them. He tells them to wait outside. As soon as the door is closed, he polls the area councilors, asking who thinks these women should be excommunicated.

Six do. The other six hesitate.

The choice is the area rector's. But he wants to be able to go out to the television cameras and say there was absolute unity in the decision to excommunicate the women. He reminds the dissenters that these women are proven enemies of the Church, hints darkly that there are other issues involved, then calls for another count.

Eight in his favor, four still hesitant.

He tells them directly there are things about these women that they don't know, things that he doesn't feel he can tell them, information that is reliable but which is of such a sensitive nature that he is not free to share it with us. He hints at lesbianism and feminism. He says that he has been contacted by somebody of importance at church headquarters and that the Church is concerned about the outcome of this court. I do not know what is fabricated and what the truth.

"That is not to say this is not a local decision," he says. "We are making this decision on our own initiative. One of our esteemed leaders might be privately convinced that excommunication is the answer, but this is absolutely a local decision. Still, it is important to know that an apostolic elder is concerned."

Eleven to one. There is one holdout.

"You don't agree that these women are guilty?" the area rector asks the councilor.

"No," he says, a younger, clean-cut fellow in a white shirt and conservative suit. He looks no different from the others, unless his tie is a little narrower.

"You don't want to please the Church?" asks Rector Bates.

"I want to please the Lord."

"To please the Church is to please the Lord."

"Tell them you can take his place," whispers a voice next to me.

I turn to see the bloody-headed man beside me.

"How did you get in?" I whisper.

"You let me in."

I raise my head. "I could take his place," I say.

The area rector looks at me a long time.

"Yes," he says. "Fochs will take his place." He says to the rogue councilor, "You're free to leave."

"I don't think you can do this," says the man.

"You let me worry about what can or can't be done," says the area rector.

"You can't expect Fochs to be an unbiased judge."

"Nonsense. Fochs is an honest man," says the area rector. "He'll listen to the spirit."

"I won't leave," the man says. He stands looking nervously about him.

The area rector stands and takes the man by the arm, starts to drag him toward the door. The man resists, slowly losing ground. The rest of the men rush to the area rector's support. They get him to the door, push him outside, close it again.

"Mark my words," says Bates. "He'll regret this someday." He wipes the sweat off his face. "Shall we vote?"

Twelve to zero.

"I will inform the women that they have been excommunicated by unanimous decision. I am proud of all of you. God is proud of you as well."

CHAPTER 16
Drive

The press has been calling, about the excommunicated women, about the two violated boys. We have to hide the paper from my oldest, keep the television set unplugged. I do not return the reporters' calls. If they manage to confront me on the way to or from the office, I refer them to the lawyer the Church has purchased on my behalf.

Feshtig keeps leaving messages on my work machine, saying he would like to speak further with me, that he felt we were making progress. He has seen the papers, he says, and knows I must be going through a difficult time. At first I have the secretary put him off gently but when he keeps calling I block his number. I know now I have told him too much.

The twins come home from school to tell my wife what the other children are saying about me. Some say their parents know I am a good man, a provost of the True Church, and that I would never do such things. Others say their parents claim I am a devil.

My wife tells me this later. The twins never mention it to me but only seem remarkably reserved in my presence.

For my wife it is more difficult than for me. She has ingrained within her too much of a sense of propriety to defend me properly.

She tells them that I have done nothing, but she knows too much to show sufficient enthusiasm. I try to keep her from the press but they get to her somehow, and everyone in the neighborhood is asking her about it as well. They are wearing her down. They are going to make her slip.

She has become a liability.

"We have to talk," I say.

"Fine," she says. "Talk."

"Just you and me," I say. "We need to get away."

She listlessly submits. We leave the children with her parents, go for a ride.

"Where are we going?" she asks.

"Nowhere. Just driving."

We drive for some time up the canyon before she opens her mouth. "I am wasting my life," is the first thing she says.

"No," I say. "It isn't like that."

"I shouldn't be with you," she says. "For my sake, for the children's sake."

"You can't leave me now," I say. "The press would eat us both alive. You need me."

She starts to cry then. I keep driving up into the mountains, paying attention only to the road.

She stops crying. "You killed that girl, didn't you?" she asks.

"You want to know?"

"No," she says. "I don't want to know."

"Why did you ask, then?"

We drive for a long time. I take the car off onto a dirt road, down through rows of pine.

"Where are we going?" she asks.

"Driving," I say. "Still driving."

I pass one that I think will do the trick, angling out toward the road as it does.

"Take me home," she says.

"I won't take you home," I say.

"Where are you taking me?"

"Nowhere."

"I don't want to be with you anymore," she says. "Let me out of the car. I can't stand being near someone like you. I hate you."

"You love me," I say. "You can't help it."

"I know you killed that girl," she says. "I can't prove it, but I know you did it."

"I didn't do it."

"I know you did!" she yells. She has begun to shake now. "I know it!"

I let her say it. I circle the car around and she makes no effort to get out. Returning in the direction we came from, the wheels spit chips of gravel all over the road. While she is shaking and her head bobbing about I reach over and press in the release button on her safety belt, carefully disengage the clip without her noticing. I let the road pass.

"I will tell you the truth," I say.

"No," she says. "Please, don't."

"I want to tell you," I say. "Lord knows I have to tell someone."

She starts screaming, her screams coming in throbs. She is shaking so hard I can feel it through the seat despite the rough road. She is half mad already. I increase the speed.

"Don't tell me!" she screams. "I'll tell, dear God, I'll tell everyone!"

"You aren't going to be able to tell anyone," I say.

I can see the angled pine. I push the gas pedal down.

"I killed her," I say. "God was beside me."

She is screaming. I drive straight at the tree, turn the wheel hard at the last moment. The car skids and starts to slide sideways. She can see it coming and I can too, and then the tree tears through the front and side of the car and the impact throws her past me and through the windshield.

Sweet Jesus, cradle me.

CHAPTER 17

Hospital

I awake gasping, my body aflame. My arm is slung out to one side, wrapped in plaster. I move my legs, feel pain tear through my back.

There is a woman above me. A nurse.

"How do you feel?" she asks.

"Not so good."

"No," she says. "I don't imagine so. The doctor will be here in a moment."

"What happened?"

"Lie back," she says, pushing gently on my forehead. "The doctor is coming."

She stands, examines the IV in the back of my hand, prods the fluid bag connected to it.

"What happened?" I ask again.

"The doctor is coming," she says. She straightens the covers and goes out.

I swallow, find my throat aching and sore. I turn my head as far as I can to one side, see beside me, in bed a few feet away, a grinning, toothless old man. He waves slowly at me.

"Not feeling well, buddy?" he asks.

I turn my head straight and close my eyes.

"Hey, buddy," says the old man. "I am asking you a question."

I turn slowly to look at him, watch as he carefully pulls off the covers, revealing a set of bowed, scabby legs. He gets out of bed and onto them, teeters over to my bed, leans over me.

"Not feeling so well today?" he asks.

"What do you think?"

"Me? I think you got what you deserved, probably. Everybody does."

The doctor comes in, pushing before him a covered table. The old man totters back to his own bed, tries to climb into it, falls to one knee, his hands flailing on the bed sheets.

"You should stay in your bed, Mr. Jenks," says the doctor, helping him off the floor. "You keep getting out of bed and we will have to put the straps on you again."

The doctor pushes the old man into the bed and covers him to the chin, then goes to the corner basin and washes his hands.

"Fochs, is it?" he asks.

"Yes," I manage to say.

"Dutch, is it? Norwegian? Originally, I mean." He comes close to me, begins to unbutton the hospital gown. "Old French? No need to answer," he says. "Still a little early yet for conversation."

Removing a stethoscope from his pocket, he presses the cold head to my chest and inserts the other ends into his ears. He sits listening, moving the stethoscope slightly, looking at something on the wall above the head of the bed.

"Weak," he says. "But better."

"He got what he deserved!" yells the old man.

"Mr. Jenks," says the doctor. "Please." He stands and pulls the curtain shut, separating Jenks off.

"Thank you," I say.

"Not at all," the doctor says. "How does the arm feel?"

"It hurts," I say.

"Good," he says. "Your head?"

He takes from his pocket a device for examining the eyes, examines first one then the other.

"It's a miracle you came out of it as well as you did."

"Out of what?"

"The accident," he says. He slips the device back into his pocket. "You haven't been briefed yet?"

"No."

"Automobile wreck up the canyon," he says. "You driving, you and your wife the only two in the car. The car rammed into a tree. You were driving far too fast, I'm afraid."

"I don't remember."

"Take my word for it," he says.

"Does my wife remember?"

"Your wife?" he asks, almost as if embarrassed. He stands up, palpates the intravenal sack. "She's dead," he says. "Didn't they tell you?"

"No," I say. "Nobody told me anything."

"Well," he says. "Now you know. I'm sorry to be so direct."

He takes a file from its rack on the door, marks something in it. He looks up.

"Are you in shock?" he asks.

"I don't know."

He comes to the side of the bed, looks into my eyes again.

"Fine," he says. "You'll be fine." He smiles in distracted encouragement. "You don't care that she's dead, do you."

"Care?"

"Why did you want to kill her?" he asks.

"What?"

"You know what I mean," he says.

"I don't," I say weakly.

He smiles, laughs. He reaches up, digs his fingers in under each side of his face, strips the face away. Underneath is the doctor from the courthouse, the man who took me by the nose.

"It doesn't matter why," he says. "All that matters is that you killed her."

"It was an accident," I say. "You said so yourself."

He pulls the portable table near the bed, uncovers it, reveals an array of knives and other instruments, most larger and harsher than one would expect for surgery. He runs his hands over them, selects the largest.

"Let's discuss this," I say.

"Why should we?" he asks. "You don't know truth from lie." But he puts down the instrument.

"Look at me," I say. "Aren't I suffering enough?"

"Enough?" he asks. "What's enough?"

He takes from the table a primed hypodermic. Pushing the needle into the intravenal bag, he depresses the plunger. I watch the liquid diffuse into the bag, quickly dispersing, the clear liquid tainted darker.

He puts on rubber gloves. He folds over the face he has torn off and ties it at the back in a knot, slips it over his mouth and nose, breathes through it. I feel my body falling slowly numb.

"Wait," I say.

"You know," he says, "it still is not too late. You can still survive."

"I admit it," I immediately say, my words thick and distant. "I killed her. I shouldn't have done it. Leave me alone."

He stays motionless for some time, then slowly shakes his head.

"I was mistaken," he says. "It is too late."

He takes up two knives, advances on me. He grabs me by the collarbone, begins to saw the blade through my chest. I can hardly feel it, but can hear it, the wet crunch of the blade as it breaks through. I pass out.

A hand and a curved needle rise and fall over my body, a length of dark thread attached to the needle grows shorter with each circuit. A length of stitching runs from my neck to my thigh. The needle knots the thread off, a face descends to sever the thread with its teeth.

It is a man whose head has been shaved, the skin below gashed and bruised, peeled back along the temples to reveal a rich, damp underflesh. He is wearing a smock. He keeps rubbing the top of his head with his free palm.

"I think we got it all back in," he says.

"What?" I ask. My voice is weak and catches on the words.

"Most of it anyway," he says. He lifts up a pan full of viscera, the integument sodden with blood. "I wasn't sure where these went. And some of them you are better off without."

I close my eyes. When I open them, he is still there.

"Remember me?" he asks. "Your old friend?"

"I took care of the doctor," Bloody-Head says. "Don't worry about the doctor. You won't be bothered by him again." He stands up and my eyesight begins to grow dim. "God loves you," he says. "Don't sell yourself cheap."

The window is open, two men in business suits peer out of it. The curtain next to me is torn down and the old man's bed is empty, his sheets spotted with blood.

I try to sit up, find the blankets have been tightened around me and tucked under. One of the pair at the window hears me struggling and comes over to place his hands on my shoulders.

The other, when he notices, takes a coil of twine from the bed-side table, ties me down.

"Comfortable?" he asks.

"People are taking a special interest in you," says the other. "People in your congregation are praying for your welfare."

"What?"

"Remember me?" asks the first. He takes out a notebook and holds it up.

"No more questions," says the second. "We promise."

They take their suit jackets off and lay them on the bed, over my belly. They start rolling up their sleeves.

"Where are we going?" I ask.

"Going?"

"We're saving you," says the second. "To the degree to which that is possible."

"Mainly we are just getting you out before you do any more harm."

They kick the brakes off the bed's coasters, begin to wheel me out.

"Wait," I say. "I'm not feeling better."

They tear off a corner of the sheet, stuff my mouth full with it, keep on. We pass through the halls, overhead lights flashing by.

"You are lucky," the first says. "Most people live to ruin themselves further."

"You won't feel a thing."

A doctor stops us in the hall, asks them where they are taking me.

"Room transfer," says the first.

"Room transfer?" asks the doctor. "That is unusual, isn't it?"

"Very unusual," says the other man. "Very unusual indeed."

"We have the papers right here," says the first, patting his pocket.

The doctor nods, watches them pass by. They push my bed forward in silence. Enter into an elevator.

"What if he had asked to see them?" asks the second. "What then?"

The first reaches into his pocket, mimes surprise. "I had the papers here a moment ago," he says. "They are around here somewhere." He smiles at the second, then down at me. "I thought it through in advance," he says.

"Where'd you learn to do that?" asks the second.

"What?"

"Lie."

"I don't know," says the first. "Picked it up somewhere. It comes in handy."

"How are you doing?" the second says loudly, shouting down at me. I shake my head.

"He's doing fine."

"He doesn't look fine."

"Doesn't matter, where he's going."

The elevator opens and they push me out toward the sliding glass exit doors. The sun is setting and the doors seem swollen with light.

"One more thing," says the first. "We need you to formally agree to this."

"Just a technicality."

"We can't let you die unless you agree to it."

"Which of course you will do."

"There is no advantage to saying no, every advantage to agreeing."

"So how about it?"

They unfurl the sheet from my mouth, like some sort of magic trick. They stand crouched above me, people streaming all around us. They seem to be waiting for something.

"So, how about it?" they ask again.

I look at both of them, turning my head from one to another. I look out the door, squinting.

"No," I say.

I choke, cough, see doctors in bloody surgery scrubs, a nurse rushing about turning knobs until the machines fall silent. I feel fingers in my mouth. There is a long hesitation as a doctor strikes my chest with a fist, and then I hear my lungs begin to breathe.

"Mr. Fochs," the nurse says. "You made it. Welcome back to the land of the living."

CHAPTER 18

Recovery

I am holding my youngest on my chest, my plastered arm preventing her from falling off the bed, my unbroken arm's hand wrapped tightly around her ankle.

My eldest is there as well, sitting in a chair beside the bed, swinging her feet, wearing her Sunday dress. The twins are beside, their hair slicked down, wearing tiny three-piece suits.

"When will you be out, Daddy?" my eldest asks.

"Soon," I say. "Very soon. The twins have been good?"

She looks up, remembering. "They were pretty good, I guess," she says.

"We were real good," says Mark. "We listened the whole time."

"Grandad spoke at the funeral?"

"Yeah," says Jack. "But he forgot what he was saying."

"He didn't forget," says my eldest. "He was crying."

Jack shrugs. "Whatever," he says.

"How did she look?" I ask.

"Grandma?"

"Mom."

"How do I know," she says. "They closed the lid."

"They had a picture of her on the top," says Mark. "The picture looked real good."

I pull my youngest back as she topples off the bed.

"Aren't you sad about it?" asks my eldest.

"Of course I am sad," I say.

"You don't seem very sad to me," she says.

"They have me all shot up with drugs."

"Drugs are bad for you, Dad," says Mark.

"Don't do drugs, Dad," says Jack.

"Medicine," I say. "It's okay. I am so crammed with medicine I can't think straight."

"When are you getting out, Daddy?" my eldest asks.

"Soon."

"How soon?"

"A few days."

The nurse comes and helps me get my legs out of bed and onto the floor. She helps me walk to the bathroom, leaves me inside for some time.

When she returns to retrieve me, she says, "You have a visitor."

She helps me out of the bathroom. In the chair nearest the bed is the area rector.

"You've had quite a run of bad luck, Provost," he says.

The nurse helps me to lie down, then goes out.

"You're all right?" Rector Bates asks.

"Not bad," I say. "Considering."

"Who has the children?"

"My wife's parents."

He nods. We sit looking at one another until the telephone rings.

"Should I get that?" he asks.

"Yes," I say. "Please."

He picks up the telephone. "Hello?" he says. "Yes. Who is calling, please?"

He holds the receiver toward me.

"Feshtig," he says. "A Doctor Feshtig. He said you'd know him."

I shake my head no. Bates pulls the receiver back to his own face.

"I'm sorry," he says. "He is unable to take your call."

I hear Feshtig frantically talking as the receiver leaves Bates' ear and is slowly replaced in the cradle.

Bates sits there a moment, seemingly embarrassed.

"I have something to show you," he says. "I don't want to shock you."

I nod.

He takes from his coat pocket a rolled newspaper, spreads it out, places it on the coverlet before me.

On the front page is the tree with my car wrapped around it. The car is folded thoroughly around the tree, the interior space reduced to nearly nothing. "Accused Molester Crashes, Wife Dead."

"It's a miracle you survived," he says. "God's looking out for you."

"How did they find me?"

"A hiker found the car. He went to the main road to wave someone down. You must have been going fast," he says. "Too fast obviously. How fast were you going?"

"I don't know," I say.

"Approximately, I mean," he says. "Take a guess."

"I don't know."

"Fast," he says. "Too fast," he says.

He stops a moment, pauses, then bows his head in a way that does not look genuine. I am much better at it than he.

"I am sorry about your wife, truly sorry."

I don't know what I should say, so I don't say anything.

"Seatbelts," he says. "Got to make sure they wear their seatbelts."

"Seatbelts," I say.

He points again to the article. "See what I circled?" he says.

I squint at the paper. "Yes," I say.

"Two certain women have been very busy," he says.

I begin to read the circled passage, slowly. I am being accused in it of all they have accused me of before. The speculation is made, on the behalf of the reporter, that perhaps when I wrecked I was trying "out of guilt and shame" to "commit suicide."

"This is appalling," I say. "I had no intention of committing suicide."

"Shameless," he says. "And so soon after the accident."

"These women," I say. "They don't care about the truth, they don't care about anything. They just want to get rid of me."

"They want to hurt the Church," Bates says, raising his voice. "The Church has been fair to them, you've been honest with them straight down the line, but they want everything their way."

"Bitter," I say.

"They take up the Devil's cause," he says.

He takes the article and folds it up, puts it into his suit pocket.

"You are the victim here, Provost," he says. "The innocent victim."

He stands up.

"I have to go," he says. "Get well soon. We are praying for you."

In a few weeks I am in a wheelchair. A few more and I crutch my way out the front door of the hospital.

The children are with my wife's parents. I come into the empty house alone. I rest for some time in the living room, catching my breath. Everything about the room, I realize, was chosen by my wife. I have had no part in it.

I go into the kitchen and open drawers and cupboards until I find a roll of plastic trash bags. I tear a few off and begin to load the living room into them. I take down the pastel, neoimpressionist Jesus, the tole-painted bears, the cross-stitch of the temple we were married in, the family photographs that she demanded I sit for with her each year. The rustic, open wallbox containing scenes and objects which she felt captured the essence of our relationship, the sheet music strewn across the piano that no one in the family can play, the cassettes of the Church's official hymns, plants with dead leaves, the best-selling books by church leaders and by those who wish to be church leaders, *The Suffering Heart*, a framed parchment depicting Jesus Christ's Anglo-Saxon face and beneath it the words "I never promised that it would be easy, only that it would be worth it."

I am shucking her whole.

There are three full trash bags and another started and the room is falling bare, but the furniture and the wallpaper still reveal hints of my wife's face. I will have them changed. I will have the room as I want it, though I don't know what I want yet.

But for now I must catch my breath.

I lie down on the couch, my damaged leg elevated. My broken arm pulses within the cast. I sleep a little.

When I awake, it is dark throughout the house. I feel better, some.

I crutch slowly through the ground floor, closing doors. In the kitchen I butter two slices of stale bread and eat them. The butter is on the verge of going rancid, slightly bitter and sharp to the taste. The rest of the fridge is empty.

I go through the newspapers piled on the table, stripping off the rubber bands, looking for news of myself. There is news of the accident, news of my wife's death and of my survival, a follow-up article on the rape of the two boys—the Church's public relations person unequivocally denying any involvement on my part, claiming, "We have investigated the matter thoroughly and see no evidence of wrongdoing." The man has not spoken to me at all and, as far as I can tell, is only taking the area rector's word on everything. There never has been—and I hope never will be—a legitimate investigation by the Church.

I spend the evening reading the newspapers backwards, I pick up the telephone and call my wife's parents, speak briefly to my eldest daughter, tell her how much I am looking forward to seeing her and the rest of the family.

I leave my crutches at the base of the stairs and pull myself carefully up. It is as much as I can manage. At the top I lie down on the floor, rest for some time before pulling myself again to my feet and down the hallway to the bedroom.

Pushing the door slowly open, I stand there swaying, legs aching. I flick on the light.

On the bed, body extended, ankles crossed, stripped of his clothes, his body broken and angled, is the bloody-headed man.

"Fochs," he says, drawing me toward him. "Welcome home."

CHAPTER 19

Threat

I awake to the sound of the telephone ringing beside the bed, the bloody-headed man holding the sheets around himself and shaking me. I stumble out of bed, striking my leg cast heavily against the bedside table, turning my leg as I fall.

The telephone keeps ringing. The bloody-headed man drags me from the floor, pulls me to the telephone, helps me pick it up.

"Hello?"

"I am looking for a Mr. Fochs."

"Fochs?" I say. "This is Fochs."

"Mr. Fochs, it has come to our attention that you may have information about a young girl's death."

"Who is this?"

He identifies himself as a detective with the Police Department.

"I already told the police everything I know."

"Your psychiatrist telephoned us," the detective says. "He claims you know more."

"My psychiatrist? I don't have a psychiatrist."

"Mr. Fochs, there is no delicate way to put this," he says. "You are a suspect."

"A suspect?"

"The things they say you did to those boys, Mr. Fochs," he says. "A man who could do something like that could murder easily enough. Not that you did them," he says. "Innocent until proven guilty."

"You can't accuse me," I say.

"Now, Mr. Fochs, who's accusing anybody? It is only what I read in the papers." I hear something rustle in the background, behind his voice. "And what I hear from your psychiatrist. We are asking for a blood sample," he says, "for comparison purposes. Just a smear test for blood type and related. If things seem to match up, we might ask for a DNA test later."

"What?" I ask. "You can't do this."

"If you didn't do it, this will clear you," he says. "If you did—"

"—I'm bedridden. I can't come down there."

"We can send someone by."

"Wait a minute," I say.

"It's for your own benefit, Fochs."

"You can't make me do it. I have a lawyer."

"Fine," he says. "You call your lawyer and work it out, friend."

"You can't make me," I say again. "I am still weak from the accident."

"Get a doctor to say that in writing."

"I have rights, you know."

"Fochs," he says. "Some name you have. Sounds like an X-rated clown. Not that I'm judging you, mind." And then he hangs up.

Bloody-Head just lies in bed, watching me. I get up and stumble around the room, throwing on my robe, then sit down on the bed again.

"Problems, Fochs?" he asks.

I dial Rector Bates' work telephone, listening to the bloody-headed man chuckle softly. The secretary asks me to hold. The Muzak starts.

"Need a helping hand, Fochs?" asks Bloody-Head.

"Leave me alone," I say. "This is all your fault."

He laughs. "It isn't anybody's fault but your own," he says. "You made the choices the whole way along."

"Hello?" says the secretary.

"Fochs for Bates," I say.

"I am sorry," she says. "Mr. Bates is unavailable. May I take a message?"

"It's an emergency," I say. "Just tell him Fochs is on the line. And that it is an emergency."

"Fochs," she says. "I don't know."

"Fochs," Bloody-Head laughs. "What the hell kind of name is that?"

"Please."

"I don't know," she says. "I shouldn't."

"It's life or death," I say. "Please ask him."

She puts me on hold.

"Get out," I say to Bloody-Head.

"Excuse me?"

"You heard me," I say. "Leave my house."

"It isn't as easy as that," he says.

"Get out!" I scream. "Get out!"

He smiles, rolls over in the bed.

I raise my arm to the square. "I command you to depart," I say.

"By what authority?"

"In the name of Jesus Christ."

He snorts, lies down. "Before, you thought I was Jesus," he says. "Changed your mind?"

"Fochs?" says the telephone. "What is it, man?"

I manage to trouble out what the police want me to do.

"So?"

"I don't want to do it. I want a lawyer," I say. "I need the Church to provide one again."

"Give them the blood sample," says Bates. "What can it hurt?"

"I don't want to give it."

"What does it matter, Fochs?" he asks. "You are innocent. This will clear you."

"But what if—"

"You are innocent, aren't you?"

I take a deep breath. "Of course I am," I say.

He hesitates a long time as if listening for confirmation from the Spirit. "I believe you," he finally says. "You wouldn't lie to me. You are telling me the truth. No lawyer then. Go through with it."

The doorbell rings downstairs. My heart is beating too fast for my chest.

"Nice try, Fochs," says Bloody-Head, "but it is never that easy."

"You can help me out of this," I say. "You've helped me before."

The doorbell rings again. "Aren't you going to answer that?" he asks.

"No," I say.

"Then I will," he says.

He stands and leaves the room. I hear the door open downstairs, hear muddled voices, footsteps on the stairs.

Two plainclothesmen come into the bedroom, hats in their hands, one blond, the other bald.

"The door was open," the blond says. "We took the liberty."

"We're here for the blood," says the bald man.

His partner elbows him. He puts on a pair of gloves. He takes a hypodermic out of his pocket, affixes a needle to it.

"I won't do it," I say.

"You got a lawyer?" the blond says. "If not, I'm going to have to ask you to come down to the station?"

I am going to tell them to arrest me but then I begin to think it over. They will have what they want in either case. If I am not arrested, I at least have a day to gather my things and leave.

I push up the sleeve of my pajamas.

"Good," says the bald one. "You are right to see it our way." He starts toward me.

"Let me go to the bathroom first," I say.

They look at each other, shrug. The bald one goes into the bathroom and rattles around the cabinets, comes back out again.

"Looks okay," he says.

"Now you're searching my bathroom," I say.

"Not at all," the bald one says, "nothing of the kind."

"Up you go then," says the blond, taking my arm, helping me to stand.

I limp my way into the bathroom.

"We'll be right here if you need anything," the blond says. "We'll be waiting."

I close the bathroom door. I strip my pajama bottoms off, my temple underclothing as well, leaving the clothing coiled around my ankle and the bottom of my cast. I lean sideways against the sink to take the weight off my injured leg. I look at my body, my pale sex slack and dull, jutting to one side.

The shower curtain rustles. I turn as if stung. There is Bloody-Head, his face taut, the X carved in his head edging dark and growing bloody again, wounds circle his skull as well.

"Need a hand?" he asks.

I close my eyes and turn away from him, hear him step from the tub to stand next to me, breathing in my ear.

"I can get you out of this, Fochs," he says.

"How?"

"Trust me," he says.

I open my eyes and look at him. "Be my guest," I say.

"I would," he says, "but first I want to know what is in it for me."

"In it for you?"

A knock comes at the door. "Hurry it up," one of the detectives says.

I glance out the bathroom window. I lick my lips.

"What do you want?"

"You know what I want."

"I don't know. I don't know," I tell him.

He shakes his head, spattering blood on the tiles. "I want you."

"I don't know what you are talking about," I say.

"You," he says. "And your daughter," he says. "Your eldest. I want her as well."

"Her soul?"

"What are you talking about?" he says. "Flesh and blood."

"No," I say. "I won't do it."

"Fine," he says. "You are going to hell in any case," he says. "I am just offering you a chance to go in style."

He goes to crouch behind the shower curtain again. I examine my bare body.

"What's taking so long in there?" asks the blond through the door.

"Give me a minute," I say.

"You've had your minute."

I pull back the curtain. "What do you mean you want my daughter?"

"Do you want to get out of this or not?"

"What will you do to her?"

"Do you really want to know?"

"As long as you don't kill her," I say. "Okay."

He stretches out his hand, asks me to take it. I take the hand, feel nothing. It is as if my hand has gone numb.

"Yourself in the bargain?" he asks.

I nod.

He gives a wide grin. He takes my hand, directs it to his crotch. I jerk my hand away.

"Go ahead," he says. "Seal the bargain."

I stay standing, looking down at him.

"You don't expect me to do this myself, do you?" he asks.

I begin to work my hand and feel him swell and grow hard as death, his tip and shaft darkening. I am caught up in his arms and thrown about and find myself bent over the sink, my legs spread. His hands touch and spread me and he is prodding me, loosening me. He drives himself roughly into me from behind. I am burning and biting my tongue and there is a slow ache. He is crushing the breath out of me. I have a feeling halfway between nausea and pleasure in the pit of my stomach. He begins spurting new blood into me.

"Where the evil has been, I will push in holy fire to burn it out," he says, grunting. "Heard that one before, brother?"

He moves faster and faster, my good leg quivering and giving, the porcelain warming, growing slippery against my belly. The detectives are at the door, knocking. The bloody-headed man sinks his teeth into my shoulder and I have to bite my lips not to cry out. I feel my whole soul tearing and flapping in the wind, and the pain welling up, and his new blood pumping through me and my old blood spattering out, until there is nothing left of me.

PART FIVE

FINISH

CHAPTER 20
A Chaste Little Kiss

My children come home. I hire a woman to watch them—a beautiful young member of the Church, a junior college girl who looks much younger. My casts come off. I regain my feet fully, go back to work. My children move smoothly past my wife's death. I regain my authority at the Church, the excommunicated women slowly fall out of attention and then disappear altogether. Everyone is happy and I am healthy, a new man. I promise the Lord I will serve him in all things. I ask him to forgive me for the faults I have, for the mistakes I have made. I receive witness that I have been forgiven.

Nothing ever comes to court. They test the sample and say it is a possible match, that they will do further tests, but never get back in touch with me. My bloody-headed friend has arranged everything.

I begin to think about taking a new wife. I owe it to my children, I owe it to myself.

My eldest daughter becomes more and more lovely each day. She is well on her way to becoming a woman.

"What is it, Daddy?" she asks when she sees me looking at her.

"Nothing," I say. "I'm just glad that you chose to come down from heaven to be part of my family."

"Oh, Daddy," she says, embarrassed. Then a few minutes later she asks, "Do you think Mommy is happy in Heaven?"

"She is," I say. "But I bet she misses us."

I come into my daughter's room at night and look at her as she sleeps. She is so lovely. If she wakes up, I don't know what I will do.

My daughter stays up late at night watching television with me. Sometimes she lets me put my arm around her and pull her close. I kiss her on the forehead, smell her hair.

"Now that your mother is gone, you're the lady of the house," I tell her. "That's a lot of responsibility."

"Oh, Daddy," she says. But I know she likes me to say it. It makes her feel important.

I buy her things, little trinkets, and leave them on the table beside her bed. She finds them and I see her privately treasure them, but she never says anything to me about them.

I can't stop thinking about her. It makes it difficult to concentrate.

"I love you," I tell her.

"Why do you keep saying that, Daddy?"

"I really love you, I guess," I say.

She lets it pass. She is pleased by the attention, but cannot see that I am courting her. I would marry her if I could, if society would allow it.

On the way home from work I see in the crowd ahead of me one of the boys from my congregation, the Bavens boy. He is drifting slowly, aimlessly, bouncing a tennis ball, a racket case slung across his shoulder. He is a handsome boy, good enough to swallow.

I follow him through the crowd, hurry to catch up with him.

"Bavens," I say. "James Bavens, right?"

He turns, startled, and sees me. "Provost Fochs," he says.

"How long has it been since we talked, Jimmy?"

"I don't know," he says. "Have we ever talked?"

"We should," I say. "We should be talking every six months. How's your spiritual welfare?"

"I dunno. Fine, I guess."

"Come by and see me."

"Well," he says. "Maybe."

"Sure," I say. "I don't bite. Tomorrow night. Nine o'clock. At the church."

"I guess," he says, embarrassed.

"You're a handsome boy, Jimmy," I tell him. "You're becoming a real man. We need to talk about that."

"I got to go."

"Sure," I say. "If you have to. See you tomorrow."

The next night he doesn't show. I am all afire with disappointment. I wait for an hour and then give up, tramp the streets home.

On the way home I pass through the woods, the moon limning everything pale and visible. I stop at the clearing where the girl died and sit on the rock. It seems a place like any other, completely ordinary.

I leave and go back home.

The children are already in bed. The babysitter sits at the dining room table with books spread all about her, writing a paper. When she sees me she starts closing the books, gathering them into a stack.

"How were the children?" I ask.

"Fine," she says. "You have such good kids, Provost Fochs."

"Thank you," I say.

She gathers her books and stands.

"No need to go so soon," I say.

"Oh," she says. "No, I have to get back."

I take the books out of her hands, put them on the table again. I lead her over to the couch.

"Come on," I say.

She sits awkwardly down on the very edge of the cushion.

"Relax," I say. "You're still being paid. Stay awhile and talk."

She relaxes a little, but not much. I ask her questions about herself, her family. About the classes she is taking in school. I inch toward her until I am very close to her indeed. I reach out and brush her hair behind an ear.

"You know," I say. "You are a very beautiful girl."

"Please don't say that," she says. She keeps shrinking back into the corner of the couch. I put my arm around her.

"Please," she says.

I kiss her. A chaste little kiss is all.

And then before I know it she is crying, trying to get her clothes back on as quickly as she can. I am not sure of all the details, but I am lying there watching her, savoring the way my body feels. My youngest is crying. The twins are at the top of the stairs looking down. I get up to put my pants on, shout at them to go to bed.

"What did you do to her, Dad?"

"Nothing," I shout. "Go to bed."

The girl is crying so hard that she can't find her way to the door. She keeps stumbling into the table. If I weren't in my own house, this would be murder number two. I yell at the twins to go upstairs and they go. I go over to the girl and take her by the arms. She shudders, tries to get away.

"Harlot," I say. "Jezebel." And thrust her out of the house.

I take a rag from the kitchen and wipe up the blood. I sit down at the table to think. Her books are there. I scoop them up and take them outside and dump them on top of her.

"Don't tell anyone about this," I say. "They will blame you." In fact around here that is generally what they do.

"And get off my porch," I say. "You can't stay here."

I go inside and close the door.

I stay downstairs a few hours, calming down. I watch the television until the national anthem comes on, but I am not tired. My skin is buzzing.

I climb up the stairs, look into each room. My youngest has cried herself to sleep. The twins are asleep as well, crouched against one another in the same bed.

Going into my eldest's room, I lean over her bed. I reach down and kiss her lips. When I lift my head I see her eyes open, watching me.

"What is it, Daddy?" she says.

I lie down beside her on the bed, kiss her again, longer, with my tongue.

"What's wrong, Daddy?"

"I don't like that, Daddy."

"Please, Daddy," she says. "Don't!"

"Daddy!" she screams. "No, Daddy, no!"

CHAPTER 21
Rebirth

The first thing Rector Bates does when I step into the office is to hit me in the face. He knocks me down, stands over me until I scramble out from under him and stand up again.

"You bastard," he says. Then he goes and sits down and holds his head in his hands.

When he lifts his head he looks all around the room, seems unwilling to meet my gaze.

"I've been a fool," he says. "I never should have believed you."

"I thought the Spirit told you to believe."

"I heard what I wanted to hear. You've used me all along, Fochs," he says.

"Have I?"

"Your babysitter called me," he says. "I went over and saw her. Jesus, what you did to her, Fochs."

"She's lying," I say.

"She's not lying," he says. "She's a twenty-year-old woman," he says. "She has no reason to lie. And those kids," he says. "They weren't lying either. The only liar is you."

"I never lied."

"You should hang for what you did," he says. "At the very least you should spend the rest of your life in jail. All those people who trusted you."

I start to protest. He raises his hand, stops me.

"You won't go to jail," he says. "The woman has agreed not to press charges. Besides, it would be too damaging for us. We've invested ourselves too thoroughly in this."

It seems to me that it is less in their interest to cover it up, but I am not in a position where I would care to say so. Instead, I smile.

"What are you smiling about?" he asks.

"Nothing," I say.

"If it was my choice," he says. Then he stands, paces rapidly, sits down again. He leans forward, places his palms on the desk. "I must respect the wishes of my spiritual betters," he says.

"Whose choice is it?"

"I can't say," he says. "My burden in this is to be obedient."

I just nod.

"Go home," he says. "Get out of here. Get out of my sight."

So I leave. So I go home.

In a few days my daughter begins to trust me again. The next time I am gentler with her. I am still provost, I still go to church every Sunday, nothing having changed except I have been forbidden by my area rector to conduct private interviews with the youth.

Still, I get a few in. An interview with the Bavens boy, for instance. He proves a good pupil, better than I would have suspected.

It goes on for a month maybe, the area rector not speaking to me at all. I have free run of the youth. My daughter and I become closer. God loves me.

Rector Bates calls me into his office again. This time he is at least civil.

"Things have been arranged, Fochs," he says. "I don't like it, but it's not my place to complain."

"Arranged?"

"Don't ask me who," he says. "I can't tell you that." He leans across the desk. "You are moving," he says.

"Moving?"

"You've been given a job," he says. "I'm not sure who has agreed to it or how many general authorities know. I know at least one does. And I respect him."

"What do you mean, moving?"

"They've arranged a job for you. At the Church College. You'll be teaching accounting. Any hint of nonsense and you're through."

I put up a show of resistance. "What if I don't like it?"

"It doesn't matter," he says. "You'll do it."

"And if I don't?"

"Then you're on your own."

I reach across the desk and shake his hand. He takes it reluctantly.

After a few minutes, I walk out of the office, whistling. I am a free man, and pure. I am on my way home to celebrate with my daughter. I have been forgiven. We are allowed to begin again, with new souls to save. We are all of us about to be reborn.

LITERATURE
is not the same thing as
PUBLISHING

Funder Acknowledgments

Coffee House Press is an internationally renowned independent book publisher and arts nonprofit based in Minneapolis, MN; through its literary publications and *Books in Action* program, Coffee House acts as a catalyst and connector—between authors and readers, ideas and resources, creativity and community, inspiration and action.

Coffee House Press books are made possible through the generous support of grants and donations from corporate giving programs, state and federal support, family foundations, and the many individuals who believe in the transformational power of literature. This activity is made possible by the voters of Minnesota through a Minnesota State Arts Board Operating Support grant, thanks to the legislative appropriation from the arts and cultural heritage fund and a grant from the Wells Fargo Foundation Minnesota. Coffee House also receives major operating support from the Amazon Literary Partnership, the Bush Foundation, the Jerome Foundation, the McKnight Foundation, Target, and the National Endowment for the Arts (NEA). To find out more about how NEA grants impact individuals and communities, visit www.arts.gov.

Coffee House Press receives additional support from many anonymous donors; the Alexander Family Foundation; the Archer Bondarenko Munificence Fund; the Elmer L. & Eleanor J. Andersen Foundation; the David & Mary Anderson Family Foundation; the Buuck Family Foundation; the Carolyn Foundation; the Dorsey & Whitney Foundation; Dorsey & Whitney LLP; the Rehael Fund of the Minneapolis Foundation; the Schwab Charitable Fund; Schwegman, Lundberg & Woessner, P.A.; the Scott Family Foundation; US Bank Foundation; VSA Minnesota for the Metropolitan Regional Arts Council; the Archie D. & Bertha H. Walker Foundation; and the Woessner Freeman Family Foundation.

The Publisher's Circle of Coffee House Press

Publisher's Circle members make significant contributions to Coffee House Press's annual giving campaign. Understanding that a strong financial base is necessary for the press to meet the challenges and opportunities that arise each year, this group plays a crucial part in the success of Coffee House's mission.

Recent Publisher's Circle members include many anonymous donors, Mr. & Mrs. Rand L. Alexander, Suzanne Allen, Patricia A. Beithon, Bill Berkson & Connie Lewallen, the E. Thomas Binger & Rebecca Rand Fund of the Minneapolis Foundation, Robert & Gail Buuck, Claire Casey, Louise Copeland, Jane Dalrymple-Hollo, Mary Ebert & Paul Stembler, Chris Fischbach & Katie Dublinski, Katharine Freeman, Sally French, Jocelyn Hale & Glenn Miller, Roger Hale & Nor Hall, Randy Hartten & Ron Lotz, Jeffrey Hom, Carl & Heidi Horsch, Kenneth Kahn & Susan Dicker, Stephen & Isabel Keating, Kenneth Koch Literary Estate, Jennifer Komar & Enrique Olivarez, Allan & Cinda Kornblum, Leslie Larson Maheras, Jim & Susan Lenfestey, Sarah Lutman & Rob Rudolph, Carol & Aaron Mack, George & Olga Mack, Joshua Mack, Gillian McCain, Mary & Malcolm McDermid, Sjur Midness & Briar Andresen, Peter Nelson & Jennifer Swenson, Marc Porter & James Hennessy, Jeffrey Scherer, Jeffrey Sugerman & Sarah Schultz, Nan G. & Stephen C. Swid, Patricia Tilton, Joanne Von Blon, Stu Wilson & Melissa Barker, Warren D. Woessner & Iris C. Freeman, and Margaret & Angus Wurtele.

For more information about the Publisher's Circle and other ways to support Coffee House Press books, authors, and activities, please visit www.coffeehousepress.org/support or contact us at info@coffeehousepress.org.

Coffee House Press began as a small letterpress operation in 1972 and has grown into an internationally renowned nonprofit publisher of literary fiction, essay, poetry, and other work that doesn't fit neatly into genre categories.

Coffee House is both a publisher and an arts organization. Through our *Books in Action* program and publications, we've become interdisciplinary collaborators and incubators for new work and audience experiences. Our vision for the future is one where a publisher is a catalyst and connector.

Praised by Peter Straub for going "furthest out on the sheerest, least sheltered narrative precipice," Brian Evenson is the recipient of three O. Henry Prizes and has been a finalist for the Edgar Award, the Shirley Jackson Award, and the World Fantasy Award. He is also the winner of the International Horror Guild Award and the American Library Association's award for Best Horror Novel, and his work has been named in *Time Out New York*'s top books.

Father of Lies was designed by
Bookmobile Design & Digital Publisher Services.
The text has been set in Adobe Caslon Pro,
a typeface drawn by Carol Twombly in 1989
and based on the work of William Caslon (c. 1692–1766),
an English engraver, punchcutter, and typefounder.